THE ASSISTANT

KATE BLACK

Chapter 1

New Beginnings

I sighed and pushed my loose blonde hair behind my ear and waited for the hostess Trish to seat my next customer. I headed for the table when my boss Mackey grabbed me by the elbow.

"Go on home early tonight Gemma. You have been here the longest and we are running slow," he said exposing his yellow teeth.

"You sure Mackey? You know I don't mind," He

waved me to go on home.

I didn't ask him again since my feet were already aching from working since noon and it was six forty five. I was a little bummed out about losing money that I could use to pay off my student loans. I had finished school almost six months ago and still couldn't find a job in the communications field. I had been working at Mackey's for four and a half years now and I loved the flexibility but it wasn't enough to pay all my bills. I headed to the bathroom to wipe the sweat off my face. I had my dark blue jeans and black Mackey's v-neck shirt on. I pulled my ponytail out of my hair and headed to the back of the pub. I waved to the other girls good night who were out smoking on their breaks and walked briskly to my car. My car was parked in a poorly lit lot that had tall bushes surrounding it. Being only 5'4 and armed with my keys only I wasn't much of a threat. I got into my little black Jetta and drove straight home to my apartment.

I grabbed my bag and told my aching feet to walk

up the stairs to my door. Each step felt like anchors attached to my calves. The closer I got to my door I could hear some animal like noises and I stopped. My hand hesitated at first but I needed to wash the smell of Mackey's fried foods and beer off me. I turned the knob and my jaw dropped. *Oh my god.* First I tried to look away from my own embarrassment but then I recognized the two naked people. My roommate Julie and Ben my boyfriend banging on the living room floor. Nothing prepares you for a shock like that. I could feel my body warm and I left myself and became some yelling sobbing girl.

"What the hell is going on?" I screamed. They both immediately grabbed for clothes to cover up with.

"I thought you were working the late shift," Ben said.

"That's all you can say. Get out now," I said balling my fist up.

I would have rather them just tell me than walk in on it. I could have sworn I was having a nightmare. Ben and I had been together for two years. Ben was supposed to be my best friend and one day my life companion. How could he even have done that? I thought I was going to marry him. Ben left the room quickly and Julie of course she had more to say. In my state of shock my roommate dropped another bomb on me.

"Look, Gemma I was going to tell you at the end of the month that Ben and are moving in together but since you caught us," Julie said hooking her bra behind her back. Julie was never anything but a roommate and someone to gossip to. She never acted interested in anything I did but was cool about the apartment.

I started to think of all the ways to tear her long brown hair out of her head but my tears and sobs were out of control.

If it were humanly possible for your brain to

explode mine would have.

"You are evicting me too," I said. She nodded her head and smiled. She slithered back down the hallway to her room.

I rushed to my room before the tears blinded me. I knew Julie was seeing someone not my boyfriend. How long have I been so blind? She did this kind of thing all the time with men. She would sleep with them and push over whomever got in her way. The only reason we were roommates is a girl at Mackey's was a friend with her and she needed a roommate and I did too.

I grabbed all the stuff my arms could carry and called my big brother Nate.

Nate was at the apartment in a matter of minutes. He told me Ben better be gone when he showed up or else he was going to kick his ass, which I was kind of hoping he would. Ben made himself scarce and left with Julie somewhere.

Thank you Julie for making me another sucker on your list.

Nate was almost five years older than me and we looked nothing alike. He was tall where I was short. I had blondc hair and he had dark brown muddy like hair. Lots of people still could tell we were siblings by our blue eyes and smile. We had the Carter shit-eating grin. Nate was always there for me when I needed him even when he went to college. He would email me or call the house to make sure I was okay. He did this after our dad decided to just leave and our mom would work two jobs.

After that night everything seemed like a blur. For the next month and a half I kept myself busy taking on the long shifts. I felt like some kind of robot. I would go home to my brother's and sleep. We didn't speak about the affair. I was hoping that with all the money I was saving from staying with him I could get a decent deposit for another place that was much smaller so I wouldn't have to get a roommate.

Summer was approaching and Mackey's finally started to pick up more business and I was working more and more. Walking out of the back room one of the other girls stopped me.

"Hey Gemma, look your ex is out front in the booth with some brunette. I poked my head out of the back room and stared at them intently digging my fingernails into my palms. They had a lot of nerve showing up here.

"Thanks for the heads up Trish," I said.

Barely paying attention to my customers my hands trembled as I eyed them planning and plotting the evil things I wanted to do to them. I headed to the bathroom to make sure I looked all right. I had lost a couple of pounds and my hair looked like hell. I adjusted my ponytail and wiped the makeup underneath my eyes clear. Smiling at them I greeted Ben and Julie.

"Hey Gemma," Ben said nervously.

"Gemma I see you finally decided to lose some weight," Julie throwing her brown hair over her shoulder with a smirk.

My eyes widened and I stormed back to the bathroom. *Don't cry. Don't cry.* I swallowed hard and forced myself back out on the floor. I stopped in my tracks when I heard Mackey call my name.

"Gemma, look I know you have gone through a hard breakup but I need your head in the game. That young lady over there says you were flirting with her boyfriend," he said pointing at Julie.

My hands immediately began to shake. Who doesn't flirt with their customers? We need the tip money.

"Mackey, I'm sorry but I wasn't flirting with anyone. That guy is my ex-boyfriend and the woman he cheated on me with. She is just trying to start stuff," I said.

"What about the other customers Gemma? They said you messed up their orders and you forgot to bring a couple of their drinks. I think I am going to have to let you go. I'm sorry I think you need to take some time to heal," Mackey said lifting my chin with his hand.

Julie was out to sabotage everything I cared for. Well, it was payback time. Leaving Mackey's for the last time I saw Julie and Ben kissing with their legs wrapped around each other by the front door. There was only one thing I could think to do. I grabbed a pitcher of beer and headed to their table.

"You guys look thirsty. How about a drink," I

said under my breath and poured the whole thing on Julie's head. I wanted to make sure I got fired for the right reason.

Two weeks of unemployment living with my big brother Nate I knew I was heading for loserville. Nate was cool for letting me stay in a small room is his apartment but I knew my days were numbered. I needed to find work and pay off my student loans. I applied for twenty jobs but I just could not find a job that would hire someone with no experience in the field. Waitressing was fast money and a great way to meet people. I knew things were getting to a changing point when Nate was asking around for me.

He was always the cool headed one of both of us and could get what he wanted with his smile. He had friends in the big leagues that he kept friends with since college. He mentioned his friend William opened a new business in security and needed a personal assistant. I had only met a few friends of Nate's since he was five years older than me. I remember William being a tall brown haired guy in his early twenties and interested in college girls and parties. Nate assured me that Will was a good guy but desperately needed help at his new side project.

"Here call my friend Will and ask him about an interview. He told me no guarantees though okay?" Nate said handing me a business card that said Campbell Security.

If I remember correctly Will was always with a girl. I'm not really surprised since Nate never brought home an ugly friend.

I punched in the number into my cell and waited to hear a voice pick up. My chest began to hurt as the seconds ticked.

"Will Campbell," a rich deep voice answered. I could barely speak.

"Hello?"

"Yes, This Gemma Carter. I am Nate Carter's

sister. He suggested I call you for a possible position with your new company," I said robotically.

"Yes glad to hear from you Gemma. Be at the address on the card around ten thirty and tell Nate no promises," he said without hesitation and the phone clicked.

I looked at my phone and even though I hadn't gotten the job I at least had an interview. I threw my phone on the counter.

"Nate, I totally got an interview tomorrow," I screamed. My brother just rolled his eyes.

"No promises though," he said.

"He said to tell you too," I said frowning. I was going to prove to William Campbell if he doesn't hire me he would regret it.

I tried to find out information about the company online so I would seem knowledgeable. It was so new and secret all I knew was it had to do with security. After I shut off my laptop I began to think about the position but my thoughts kept me wondering what Will looked like. I was weary of being a personal assistant since I have never really worked in an office since my teens. Something about being in an office all day sounded boring. I fell asleep that night worrying about what to wear the next day.

The next morning I dressed in my best black business slacks with a matching blazer and a white long sleeve button up blouse. I wore black heels to give me some height. My makeup was light except my red lipstick. I had read in a magazine that red was a power color and I was notorious for wearing it. I wanted to start this interview with a clean slate. I wanted him to think I could handle anything he threw in my direction. I refused to be the weak girl who had lost her job and boyfriend living with her big brother.

It took only a few minutes from the busy city to reach his house. My jaw dropped when I realized the address on the card was Will's home address. I drove my beat up black Volkswagen up to a gated property with security. I hit the button and a voice asked me who I was. I replied that I was Gemma Carter here for the job interview. The brass gates slowly opened up revealing a lengthy paved driveway. I was already feeling out of place but if this job paid half as much of what I thought it could I would be okay. I parked in front of the stone mansion that could fit three or four of my old family's house inside it. I checked myself in the rear view mirror before attacking my interview. I flattened my hair back taming the crazy pieces and checked for lipstick on my teeth. My stomach began to ache the closer I got the house. I took a deep breath and reached for the doorbell. The door opened suddenly and I let out a small shriek. An older man in a suit with gloves greeted me.

"Ms. Carter," the older gentleman said waving me in. "Master Campbell will see you in the study," he said. I felt like I was in the movie Clue with "Master Campbell will see you in the study" comment.

So William Campbell had a butler and he was interviewing me in his private home. My chest tightened from just how unusual this interview was starting.

"Thank You sir," I said. I tried hard to stay confident when I spoke but it was clear I was in way over my head. This guy had to be swimming in dough to have so much hired help.

The butler escorted me to a room that was filled with walls of books and beautiful leather chairs. The chairs were seated nicely in front of a mahogany desk. I sat at the edge of the leather seat looking around the room at the books. Time seemed to be passing slowly and I looked over my resume a few times to make sure I had everything he might need including my references. My palms were sweating and I began to shake my leg.

I heard a deep voice muttering to the butler outside the study. I took the opportunity to straighten out my shirt and dust off my pants. The door opened and the one and only Master William Campbell came in the room without looking at me. He took the seat behind the desk and looked over some papers. I sat there wondering if he was going to speak to me or acknowledge my existence. I couldn't keep my eyes off of him he was gorgeous. His brown hair neatly cut and his shirt hugged his body. He wore dark slacks with a blue shirt that was loosened around the collar. That is when I cleared my throat as lady like as possible. I was determined to get his attention.

His rich blue eyes that his shirt brought out peered up from his papers and stared at me.

"Ms. Carter, after reviewing your resume I see

you have a communications degree," Mr. Campbell said with a slight smile.

"Yes, I just graduated this year," I said trying to keep my posture straight.

"Did your brother tell you exactly what the job you're interviewing for is?" He asked.

"My brother Nate said it was for a personal assistant," I said.

"Ms. Carter, May I call you Gemma?" he asked.

"Yes," I said nodding.

"You are a young woman and I understand you probably have a social life but, this job entails some long hours. What I like to do is for you to review the details about the job and tell me if you are interested," William said. "Do you have any questions so far?" he asked.

I smiled and scanned job description, "On your description you have the assistant would live on the property, would that come out of my salary?" I asked.

"Gemma, part of the job requires that you be close enough to me without crowding too much. You will have major holidays off paid," he said clasping his hands in front of him.

"So, if you don't mind me asking where would I be staying?" I asked.

"There is a guest house on the property or you can have a room on the opposite wing of the house. I want you to look it over and call me if you are interested or you have any other questions," he said handing me his business card.

"By the way when is the earliest you can start if you consider taking the job?" he asked getting up from his desk.

I didn't want this interview to be over. I wanted to look at him some more. I hesitated for a moment and replied, "As soon as possible." I smiled and held out my hand for him to shake it. He gave me a sturdy grip and I squeezed back showing him I was no princess.

"Thank you for your time Mr. Campbell. I really do appreciate it," I said smiling.

"Gemma, call me Will and hopefully I will be hearing from you soon," he said holding the door open for me. I looked deep into his eyes and could not help wanting that job right then and there. I kept my composure and got back into my sad looking car and drove back to Nate's apartment.

I read and reread the job description. He wasn't asking for anything crazy. He wanted someone to keep tabs on birthdays, send cards, set up meetings and vacations, and sometimes I could even tag along to make sure he was on task. Nate seemed a bit wary about me moving into his house but, the pay was great and Nate knew William since college.

"Gemma, Will is a good guy. Do me a favor though, do not mess this up. This opportunity to make this much money does not just come along," he said patting me on the shoulder.

"So you think I should take it?" I asked.

"Of course, you are not going to make that much with room and board anywhere else. Plus, Will likes to help people out or he would not have interviewed you on such short notice," Nate said.

"Wait, so he is hiring me because you asked him to?" I asked. All the excitement I felt just got kicked right out of me.

"No, he only said he would interview you. He said there was no promise of hiring you," Nate said. "But, I should warn you that Will is a ladies' man so, don't get all hot and bothered by him,"

I rolled my eyes and punched Nate in the arm like when we were kids. He must have known I thought he was cute or something. He definitely wasn't the same college guy that ignored me at my parents. I shook it off and went over the job description.

I really had no other options so I made my

decision and called Mr. William Campbell. The phone rang only a few times.

"Mr. Campbell, This is Gemma Carter calling about the job," I said. My voice was trembling. I couldn't believe I was doing this. I was going to take a job that requires me to move into a mansion with a handsome employer. It was the closest adult decision I had made since I got out of my relationship with Ben.

"Gemma, again please call me Will," he said. "Have you decided if you want the job?" he asked.

"Sir, I mean Will, I accept the job. I can start Monday if that is fine with you," I said swallowing hard. My sweaty hands almost dropped the phone

"That sounds great. I will send my butler Charles and a few guys to get your stuff Monday after you arrive. I will show you the agenda for the day and you can play everything else by ear," he said. I could almost hear him smiling.

"Sounds great, I will see you Monday then. Have a good weekend sir," I said.

"You too Gemma, until Monday then," he said and the phone went dead.

I looked up at Nate who was eaves dropping waiting to hear what was going on.

"I move out Monday and start my new job as a wealthy personal assistant," I said jumping up and down.

"You know I would normally celebrate but, I have a date and I cannot be late," Nate said patting me on the back.

"Oh, that is totally cool with me," I said. "I will probably just start packing up and stuff," I said. "Just so you know I will pay you for letting me stay and helping me get the interview," I said.

"Gemma, don't worry about that. That is what big brothers are for," he said hugging me.

In the blink of eye he was gone to get ready

for his date. Lately, I was kind of jealous that he went out and I was stuck feeling sorry myself. Granted with my new job I won't be able to go out very much but I have some wonderful eye candy to taunt me or drive me mad.

The weekend crawled and I found myself not sleeping and waking up around three o'clock in the morning. I kept having dreams about catching Julie and Ben. How smug she was when I caught them. I guess my heart was still hurting from it and this change is what I needed.

Monday came around and I took what belongings would fit into my car and left the rest to the butler Charles. I gave my brother Nate one last hug before moving out. "Thank You for everything," I whispered. He whispered back you're welcome.

"Call me later and let me know how things are working out," Nate said. "Plus, I will be in touch with Will to see how things are for him,"

"Don't make me look stupid though," I said.

I drove to my new fancy job and place I would call home for a while. I rang the doorbell and Will opened it. "You don't need to ring Gemma. Let me help you with those boxes. We have a lot of work to do today," he said. "Upstairs on your left pick which room you would like, you are going to stay in the main house right?" he said grabbing most of the boxes in his arms.

I was caught off guard but I didn't see the harm in staying on the opposite side of the house considering it was a mansion. I pointed for the opposite wing of the mansion.

I stared at his butt as he walked away with my boxes up the stairs. Will was wearing a pair of dark jeans and a fitted t-shirt. Even, when he tried to look like he was slumming it he was a super model. *Brain, stop being such a whore. This is your boss. Stop checking him out.*

I ran up the lengthy flight of stairs following him and took a left at the top railing. Three bedrooms were unoccupied for my picking. I opened the first door on the right. The room had dark red walls and seemed depressing. The bedding matched with the gold posts. Something about the room did not sit well with me. I could feel the impending doom in this room for some reason. I left and ventured to the next room and it was set up the same as the first one but different colors. The colors were silvers and greens. The colors were pretty but I still was not sure so, I had to check the last room. I turned the brass handle to the last door and the room spoke to me. Purple, the room was decorated in purples and silvers my favorite color.

"This is it," I breathed out.

I walked over to the window and stared out it. The view was stunning. There was a pool and a garden maze with roses. It reminded me of Alice in Wonderland. Flowers of different colors splashed the greenery, it was hypnotizing. I had completely forgotten Will was holding all my boxes patiently when I heard him clear his throat.

"I see you chose the purple room," Will said.

I nearly jumped out of my skin. I did not hear him with all the excitement I was having. I threw my belongings that I was holding on my new bed.

"Shall we get started for today or would you like to take a few minutes to get acquainted with your new quarters?' Will asked.

I smiled and felt the need to help my new amazing employer. I chose to check out the new job and check the rest of the house out.

I followed him down the hall carefully watching him walk again. He showed me around to his room that was at the other end of the hall. It was grand but he didn't lead me any further inside. I saw his king sized bed with gray satin sheets and comforter. He closed the door and led me back downstairs where he showed me the kitchen, dining hall, rooms for meetings and the rest of the help. The help stayed on the first floor of the mansion. He never showed me their rooms out of respect of their privacy.

He then walked me to the study where we had our first meeting.

Chapter 2

Confused

"Gemma, here is a general list for the day," Will said handing me a paper. The words were in bold letters and colons. Was he serious? The list entailed:

Bring me my morning coffee

Call hotel and airline for travel

Send fax to clients that have pending payments

Send out emails for follow-ups

Take suits to the cleaners

Get slideshow ready for next week's conference

Get any mail from the Baltimore office

Keep the Baltimore office in the loop of conferences

I read it over and seemed pretty easy but I still couldn't understand why I needed to be here twenty-four hours a day. I could easily do this and leave but I wasn't going to bite the hand that feeds me.

Will was a very intense man. He stared at his computer while I checked over the list.

"Well, maybe you should get started on the list," he said never looking at me.

As I left the room I could feel his eyes on me. Part of me was hoping I was not imagining it. I couldn't help to smile as I left and found my way to the kitchen.

I started by getting him and I both a coffee. The problem was I had no idea how he liked his coffee. I tiptoed back down the hall where Will was in his office on a heated phone call. His back was turned to me looking out the window. His body language told me that he was a man who didn't like to be argued with. He stood erect and his voice was strong and he never stumbled on a word. When he turned and faced me his jaw was tight. I could tell he was not pleased to see me.

"Get me the numbers I asked for and get back to me," he said placing his phone on the desk hard.

"Err, I got you a coffee but, I didn't know what you like in it," I said afraid to say too much. His demeanor was frightening. He then sat down in his chair and pointed for me to sit.

"Gemma, thank you for the coffee. I like it with sugar and cream. Also, I thought I should mention not to disturb me when I am on business call. My job can be very stressful and I get very agitated quickly and I would hate for you to be in the wrong place at the wrong time," he said rocking back and forth in his chair.

Something about his words scared me. I gave a half smile and apologized. This job was weirder by the minute. "Excuse me, but why do you really need me here? Why not do this at your office?" I asked. I could not believe I was asking him this now. I could possibly lose my job asking a crazy question.

"I was wondering when you were going to ask me that," he said with a smile.

"I need some stress taken off me. In both my personal life and work. I try to stay away from the main office as much as possible. I may ask you to go to the office and get things for me," he said. "Did you read everything that was on the list? You may have to go to events with me,"

"I thought that was for girlfriends and wives," I said. I was starting to feel like a prostitute or gold digger. I bit the inside of my cheek trying to figure out what this was about.

"Look, I know I can get a woman but, I am not interested in anything serious. However, if I need arm candy without the drama, that is where you come in. Plus, I will purchase your clothes if needed, now you can understand my deal with working from home a little better" he said trying to reassure me.

I shifted myself in my chair and said, "I do not want to sound ungrateful for the position but aren't you looking for a prostitute?"

Will let out a chuckle and got up from behind his desk. "Gemma, most women find me intimidating. I hired you because I knew you needed this job and you would do your best. In no way do I want you to feel like some whore. In this line of work I need people who can do their job and keep their mouths shut. You have the credentials just not the work experience. I don't want to go to the office due to some drama I avoid at all costs," he said taking the seat next to me.

I still did not feel at ease about it but there was nothing sexually going on. In one way I was kind of flattered that he thought I was eye candy.

"I am not going to lie sir, I really do need this job. I will do my best and help ease the tension," I said reassuring him with a fake smile.

"Good, I will be out of town next week and I will leave you a list of things I will need to get done. Mostly, I need you to be ready for a charity ball when I return. You will be meeting my colleagues for the first time and they will be asking you a lot of questions about my business. Your job will be to tell them nothing. This line of work in security is to be kept discreet and not public. They want to know my secret to success and they will try anything. I mean anything," he said.

I nodded and got up and went back to work down the hall. I worked mostly on a laptop that he provided for me. I worked until lunchtime. I walked down the hall and checked in on Will. He was hard at work on his computer. I knocked lightly on the door.

"Sorry, but I just wanted to make sure you did not need any lunch?" I asked. I tucked my loose hairs behind my ear.

"Charlotte the cook will bring me something later. How are things going with today?" he asked barely looking up at me. I don't think I had met Charlotte yet. She must have been told to keep her presence unknown.

"Umm..They are going great. I just need to finish setting up a few meetings and travel arrangements for you and you are good to go for next week," I said.

He kept his head down and he continued to type not acknowledging my answer. I walked back to the kitchen opening the refrigerator to look for some food. The woman Charlotte he was referring to startled me and I dropped a bottle of water. It busted open and my face turned crimson.

"Sorry, I am just trying to get used to everything and I have a case of butterfingers," I said jokingly.

"It's okay darling, I will clean it up. So, you are the new assistant?" she asked arching her brow.

"Yeah, I'm not sure how well things are going yet. I feel like I am more of an annoyance than anything," I said.

"Mr. Campbell has a hard exterior but, he is a great giving person," Charlotte said.

I wondered why he had to be so tough and keep secrets. So, I did what any nosy person would do I asked questions to the people who knew him the best.

"Does Mr. Campbell ever go to his office?" I asked.

"Occasionally, he does. He likes his privacy Ms.?" Charlotte said,

"Sorry, I am Gemma Carter," I said holding out my hand to shake.

She shook my hand. Her hands felt rough and worked. Charlotte wore a uniform that looked like my best interview outfit. She wore dark slacks and a white button up shirt. Her hair was pinned away from her face in a bun. She was still a very pretty lady even though wrinkles had embellished her skin. She knew a lot about Will and I knew I had to befriend her to find out more information. I spoke to her a little more about where I came from while she made lunch for Will.

"Do you want me to take that to him for you?" I asked. I knew I had pressed my luck when she gave me a sour look.

"You better eat your lunch. Sounds like you will be busy today," she said leaving the room with a tray of food for Will.

I ate my food in the kitchen by myself looking out the window. For some reason being around Will made my heart still hurt from my ex boyfriend Ben having an affair with Julie. I kept trying to figure out what I did that was wrong or what I could have done better. I could almost feel the pain in my chest as I remembered him on the floor with Julie while they thought I was working. *What if I hadn't caught them that night? What would have happened?*

"Penny for your thoughts," Will said.

"Oh," I said startled. "Sorry, I was just thinking of somebody I used to know," I said.

"Want to talk about it?" He asked. "You look like you might cry," Will said.

"Oh, no. I'm fine," I said. I distracted myself and cleaned up my dishes. "Sometimes I just get lost in my thoughts,"

"I have your meetings set up for the rest of the week. Your driver has been notified of what time to get you," I said washing my hands off.

"Great. I know this is a weird job situation but, if something is bothering you please let me know as soon as possible," he said. His brow creased and he stared at me again with those deep blue eyes. I would definitely give lots of pennies for those thoughts. He had major mood swings. My first day should have been a warning that he would be difficult to work with. He seemed to move from cold and distant to warm and caring.

Charlotte was right though he was very giving most of the time.

The days went on like that and I felt more isolated from the world. I took every opportunity to go out to get things for him. Will kept himself withdrawn most of the time. He was either in his study or at his office. I hadn't made any personal calls but I started to slip and text Nate. Thank god for cell phones. What was life like before them?

Everything was taking a toll on me. I was super nervous, wasn't sleeping very much, and not being a very good employee.

After the first week I started making the room my own and got some lavender to help with my insomnia. The weekend finally came and I went to the store and bought a little décor to put my touch on the room. The bed was the most fabulous thing about my room. It was like sleeping on a cloud. The bed hugged my body each night but it wasn't enough. I needed to exercise or read to relax.

The weekend dragged. I spent most of it doing random chores for Will and getting him ready for his trip even though I was technically off. I was downstairs in a spare room he set up as my office when I heard him yelling my name. I came running out of my make shift office. I couldn't find him. I ran by the staircase when I realized he was calling from upstairs. I ran up the stairs fast almost tripping. He was in his bedroom.

The doorknob was also brass like mine. I

turned it and pushed the door open. I stood there gasping in awe. His room was spectacular. He had mod furniture placed nicely throughout the room. I remember his king size bed with silver bedding from the first day. The windows overlooked the front and the back of the property. I looked around to find him by listening for his voice. It was coming from another room. He was behind double doors that I slowly opened

"Sir, are you calling me?" I asked keeping my eyes to the floor. I had only seen a few guys naked and it still made me blush.

I heard him laughing. "Jesus, Gemma I am dressed. I need some help with my tie and I need your opinion on some jackets for this conference," he said.

I raised my head up and looked around. I felt like a little girl after that. I circled the hangers in the biggest walk in closet I had ever seen. I am pretty sure he could rent it out to a small family. I also noticed how great of shape

Will was in with his shirt open and unbuttoned. I tried not to let him notice I was checking him out again.

I pointed at the suits I thought would look most flattering on him and what would demand attention in the room. I picked a dark suit with light shirts and solid ties. While I did that he buttoned up his shirt.

"Thanks Gemma, You are a life saver now help me with this tie," he said in front of a full-length mirror.

My hands shook as I tried to tie his tie. I had to stretch on my toes to reach him. He was clearly a foot taller than me. "Sorry, It had been a long time since I had to help a man with his tie," I said. I bit my lip as I concentrated. His smell was intoxicating and his hair was a bit unruly. What was wrong with me? I wanted to jump my boss. I needed to get a grip. Then out of the blue he said something strange.

"You know you shouldn't wear such dark lipstick," he said as he watched me fixing his tie.

I stopped and looked at him. "Why?" I asked. I was offended like he was calling me ugly.

"Men will be scared to kiss you," he said looking right into eyes.

My face warmed and I laughed. "Well, I don't think I need to worry about that," I said. Kiss me please Kiss me my body was throbbing for him. I moved back to fixing his tie. He looked at me and laughed.

"What is so funny?" I asked. Did my breath stink? Did I have a booger hanging out of my nose?

"Nothing," he said with a wicked smile.

"I wanted to let you know I will be back on Wednesday. Thursday will be the big charity event. My driver Stan will take you to get a dress. Tell him where and when and he will be ready to take you. I left you a credit card to get what you need," he said with a side smile.

I moved in a little closer to him as I finished tying his shiny black tie when I felt his manhood against me. He was looking in the mirror then right to me. I bit my lip and stepped back so he could see his self in the mirror. He grabbed my hand lightly pulling him back to him. What was happening?

"Thank you," he said. "You are a real life saver. Go have fun this week and visit your brother. Also, keep your phone with you so I can touch base with you about upcoming meetings and email and such," he said

Back to business I guess. I slowly walked back downstairs. How was I going to work knowing my boss is this hot and I sleep in the house with him? He intentionally asked me to help him with that tie. God, he was going to be the death of me.

Most of the week went by routinely and I tried not to think about the incident in the closet. I tried to hang out with my brother Nate but he was busy with his job and some girl he had been dating. I finally got the nerve to go shopping for the charity event. I found a purple silk halter dress that hugged my curvaceous body in the right places. The price tag had way too many zeros but I was doing this for work. I found some cute silver heels to match. The hardest part was getting a makeover. I went to a salon downtown and got the works. My hair was cut and colored. I got waxed and a facial. I never thought beauty would be such a pain in the ass. I looked in the mirror at the salon and saw a new person. Somebody I wanted to see again.

Stan drove me back to the mansion where I was working. I brought my new things up to my room when my phone rang. Will was calling me. I picked up and said hello.

He barked over some orders and asked me to change his flight for tomorrow for tonight on a red eye and hung up. He was in a bad mood and stayed short with me on the phone.

My fun was officially over. I worked on his tickets for a few hours and got him back tonight. I called him and sent him his flight plan via email. He sounded stressed out. His answers were short and assertive. Then again he was the boss of his own company and that can be very strenuous on one person I reminded myself.

That night I awoke to Will talking to someone. I peeked out of my bedroom and saw him with a woman. It was validation he was not gay and that he did let women into his home besides the help. She was beautiful. She had dark brown curls that lay on her shoulders. I watched them head back into his bedroom. I slowly snuck back into my bed wishing that were I. Instead, I was just the ugly help with the disgusting red lipstick. I lie on my bed looking at the moon that was shining through the window. Most women my age would have gone after Will. Why hadn't I. Maybe this was the reason behind me losing Ben to another girl. Then the strangest thing happened. I got a text message from

Ben.

-I am sorry about Julie. It was a mistake.

That is all he could say. I felt like calling him and telling him how lame he was. Why did I bother wasting four years of my life with a loser? I chose to take the upper hand. I did not reply back to him. I was assuming he was drunk texting or Julie broke up with him. Either way I was better than that. I was now a businesswoman making great money.

Chapter 3

Oops

I got up the next morning for work forgetting about Will's lady friend. I showered and dressed and made my way to the kitchen for some coffee. I was still steaming about Ben when Will's lady friend came in wearing Will's dress shirt. Her eye makeup was smeared across her face. She looked like hell. I gave her a smile and offered her some coffee.

"So, who are you the cook or the maid?" She

asked with a nasty tone.

Part of me wanted to throw my coffee on her and part of me felt sorry for her. I knew I would be staying here with Will tonight and she wouldn't. So, the joke was on her.

"No, I'm his assistant. If you don't mind I have to get to work now," I said smiling. Boom. Man did that feel good. One for me and zero for the skank. I walked into my office with my head held high and got to work on setting up meetings for next week.

I jumped when I heard a knock at the door and I raised my head to see Will standing in the doorway. I looked through my lashes at him.

"Is everything ok Sir?" I asked.

"Did you say something rude to my friend this morning?" he said leaning against the doorframe.

"No, she asked me if I was the cook and I told her I was your assistant," I said with a coy smile.

"In the future play nice with my friends. Your job counts on it," he said walking away shaking his head.

What the hell did that mean? I don't want to be friends with his groupies. I got through the day without talking to Will but not by choice. I was inundated with work so I stayed at my desk most of the day. I sent him emails only and left him alone. *What was he trying to do to me?* I was starting to feel incredibly lonely and couldn't wait for some action. I needed to get away from the house and Will. I kept thinking how different life was when I worked at Mackey's.

Will came back into my office and asked if I was okay. I assured him I was fine. It was five o'clock and the event started at eight thirty. I was excited about breaking the monotony and getting out of the house.

"What time do you need me ready tonight?" I asked Will.

"Gemma, I forgot to tell you I am going to take my friend Liza tonight. I am sorry about the last minute notice," he said with a fake smile.

I could feel my eyes welling up and the pain of rejection hit my chest again. I basically was starting to feel good about myself and he took it away again.

"That is fine, I will return the dress and shoes then," I said and looked back at my computer. *Don't cry Gemma. Don't cry Gemma.*

"Oh please don't take back the dress and shoes. You will definitely need them for future events," he said tilting his head to the side. "You sure you okay?" he asked one more time.

"I'm totally fine," I said swallowing a hard bubble of rejection.

He stood there for a few moments while I pursed my lips together and kept working pretending like everything was great. I was giving my boss the silent treatment because I was a child and terribly jealous of Liza now. He left the room and got ready for the charity event. I finished up a few things and headed towards my room for the evening. I had a date with the TV and some good snacks. I pulled my hair down from my ponytail and brushed the knots out of it. I lie on my bed rubbing my temples. I wanted to cry over the fact he had chosen her against me. Liza was different than me by a long a shot. She was completely opposite of me. She had dark hair and long legs. She exuded sexiness. I could barely get my makeup right according to Will. I closed my eyes and heard Will calling me from his room again.

I let out a sigh. "Now what?" I said under my breath. I stomped down the hallway to the East wing of the mansion.

I entered his room and I began to get sick. I couldn't even look at his bed knowing what he just did with Liza in it. I was so jealous and I wanted to be Liza tonight but I would have to just deal with it and suck it up.

"Will, you called for me?" I said politely.

"I need help with my tie again," he said as he stood in front of the mirror.

I walked slowly behind him and he turned and looked at me. "I am sorry about tonight. I will make it up to you," he said.

"Oh, no big deal. I got a big date tonight anyways," I said smiling. I was trying hard not to look pathetic.

"With whom?" he asked. His jaw clenched. If I didn't know better he was getting jealous.

"His name is the television. I plan on hanging out with him until I get tired and bored. You know like most relationships?" I said with a smile.

"I see you listened to me about the lipstick," he said.

"Kind of. I was getting ready to relax when

you called me in here," I said.

"Your hair looks beautiful down," he said. He rubbed his fingers through it. I could feel tingles throughout my body. I never felt a spark like I did when he touched me. I could feel my body warming and I tried to keep my eyes on his tie.

I tried to change the subject. "I wanted to thank you for letting me get a makeover and buying me a dress for tonight but, things got weird I guess. I should be nicer to your lady guests," I said biting my lip.

Will had removed his fingers from hair and was watching me attentively. Once I stopped talking he said, "Gemma, You are killing me."

"Sorry, what did I do wrong," I asked.

He reached his arms to me pulling me in closer to him. He placed his lips over mine and moved his tongue in my mouth. I rubbed my fingers through his hair. My body yearned for his. He pushed me against the wall letting out a deep groan through his mouth. His mouthed tasted better than I imagined. His lips felt like silk rubbing across mine. I rubbed my hands over his biceps feeling the ripples of muscles beneath his shirt. He picked me up and wrapped my legs around his waist.

"Master Campbell, your car is ready," yelled Charlotte from outside the bedroom.

We both stopped and looked at each other. My hair was disheveled and his shirt was open.

"Ugh, Thank you Charlotte, I will be right there," He said smiling at me. He gently placed me back onto my feet. He licked his lips like I was chocolate left over on his face.

I quickly helped him finish getting ready not speaking to him. My face felt hot and my finger shook from adrenaline.

"Sorry Gemma, that shouldn't have happened and I promise I won't do that again," he said buttoning his cuff.

My shoulders fell and I knew I would never be anything like Liza. I would always be an assistant. Tears filled my eyes and I stormed out the room down the hall to my own room.

"Gemma, wait," Will said.

I shut the door and locked it behind me. I sat against the door crying like a teenager when I was mad at my parents. I sobbed into my hands until I heard him leave. How could I be so weak? He was my boss I should know better than to mix business with pleasure. Feeling disappointed in myself I finally got myself off the floor and onto the bed. As I lay there on the bed, I had an epiphany. The one thing that was common about my relationship problems was me. I was at the root of all it. I needed to not show my feelings anymore. I needed to toughen up. I was not going to be anyone's second best. I contemplated leaving my job but I felt like I was being weak.

Instead, pulled myself together and went downstairs and grabbed a beer out of the fridge.

It would only take a couple for me to feel a buzz since I was a lightweight. I hadn't been drunk since my first year of college. Charlotte walked into the room and gave me an appalling look.

"Ms. Carter, what are you doing?" she asked. She picked up my bottles and placed them in the recycling bin.

"Feeling sorry for myself, oh and don't worry I will clean those up," I said waving to my mess of bottles that surrounded me.

Charlotte still cleaned behind me. Then she did the unthinkable. She grabbed a beer and sat down with me. She put her feet on the chair in front of me. I couldn't help but to smile.

"Charlotte, can I ask you something?" I asked.

"Sure, I am not sure if I have any answers," she said peeling the label from the beer bottle.

"Master Campbell, Will, Why did he hire me?" I asked. Tears flooding my eyes and I let out a sigh.

Charlotte did not answer immediately. She took in a deep breath and let it out.

"Gemma, Can I call you that?" she asked. I nodded.

"Master Campbell, he is a very successful man. Naturally, women flock to those who have a comfortable future. I think when he interviewed you he knew that you actually appreciated the job and him," she said rubbing her tired hands.

"You make it sound like I interviewed for his girlfriend," I snorted.

"I didn't say that but, anyone who works with Master Campbell needs to have impeccable certitude. Believe me he does extensive background checks on employees. He has had to deal with a lot of drama from the ladies," she said.

"I guess I should feel grateful but, sometimes I feel like he can be bipolar," I said.

Charlotte let out a little chuckle. "I have

been working for him since he was in his late teens and early twenties," she said now looking out the window.

A set of headlights was shining up the long driveway. I shooed Charlotte down the hall and I whispered, "Thanks for the girl talk."

"Get to bed," she mouthed back as she walked fast down the hallway to her room.

I managed to clean up the bottles we left out on the table before the door opened. I was immediately sober when I heard Liza's annoying laugh. I rolled my eyes and pretended to be busy doing something important in the kitchen. I prayed that they would not notice my presence. I saw Will heading up the stairs holding his hand out for Liza and she followed. Her eyes caught mine and she gave me a little wave and a smirk. Well, played whore well played.

An hour went by and I decided I could probably head to my office and work on last minute things.

My heart could not find the courage to go upstairs. I did not want to be close enough to hear them. I knew it would be a long night and the beers were starting to make me drowsy. I curled up on the little love seat that was in my office.

My mind replayed the earlier events. I could just quit and find another job, I could get a lawsuit against Will for sexual harassment, and I could stay and endure it. I voted against the lawsuit since I wanted it too. I wanted him naked in that closet bad. I fell asleep on that little cramped love seat.

I awoke to Charlotte covering me with a blanket. My head still felt fuzzy.

"What time is it?" I asked. I grabbed my head and tried to prop myself up.

"It is eight in the morning," she said.

"Shit," I said under my breath. I ran up the stairs and grabbed a shower and readied for the day.

I ran back down the stairs to my office where my phone was ringing. The caller id flashed Ben's name. My fingers hovered over the answer button. If I answer this I will be the weak one again. He will just find another person to sleep with and hurt me.

I hit the button and made my phone go to voicemail. I tried to look busy before I heard Charlotte bringing Will his coffee. I emailed him all his meetings and travel arrangements for next week. I also sent him an email asking for some personal time. I watched for Charlotte with her tray heading down the hall of doom. I know he wouldn't answer me until he got his coffee. He couldn't work until the caffeine was pumping through him plus, he had a long night with Liza.

While I waited my phone alerted me that I had a voice mail. I knew it was Ben he was being relentless with his calls. I hit the button to listen to his message. I placed the phone to my ear and the sound of his voice sent all the feelings back to the night I caught him and Julie. It was his apology. The whole I never meant to hurt you and I would love to apologize in person. I dropped my head to my desk and let out a sigh.

Chapter 4

Fired up

I sat at my desk and pondered the thought of the reasons why Ben cared enough to apologize. *Why did it matter?* Julie met the needs he required. While I was deep in thought I heard Will yelling my name in an angry tone.

I ran down the hall to his office, scared that he was angry with me. His jaw was tight and he pointed for me to sit in the leather chairs.

"Gemma, I need you to rearrange all these

meetings and my travel arrangements. You made some real major errors on these. You know I am running a company here don't you?" he said scolding me.

I pursed my lips together and shook my head yes. "Sorry Sir, I will get right to it," I said leaving the room.

I couldn't believe his split personality. He was Jekyll and Hyde. I spent the rest of my day fixing his meetings with the big wigs in New York and California. I also sat on the phone fighting with the airlines to refund his tickets and get his new flights arranged to his liking.

Later that evening I sent over his new itineraries and the new meeting line up. My shoulder pinched as I waited for him to yell at me since; he was so good at that. My inbox lit up with an email that was another charity event and they really would like to have Will present a speech there. I forwarded it to Will not really looking into the email afraid of his rejection again.

I shut down my laptop and was about to head for the kitchen for some water when I gasped for breath. Will was standing against the doorframe. His eyes were dark and looked tired.

"Is everything ok Will?" I asked.

"We need to talk," he said.

Here it is. He was going to fire me for messing up the meetings and travel arrangements.

He waved me to his office. I followed behind him and he closed the door behind him. I swallowed hard and my palms began to sweat. He pointed for me to sit and he took the brown leather chair beside me. He crossed his legs and let out a small sigh. *Here it comes.*

"Gemma, I need to apologize for my behavior yesterday and today. What I did was inappropriate and I really don't want to lose you. You are really good employee and I hope we can start fresh," he said.

I was taken aback for a minute. "I understand you have been under a lot of stress lately but, as far as yesterday, maybe I should just take a few days off. I think I might have been getting mixed signals," I said.

He rubbed the back of his neck. He was feeling bad about the other night. He felt bad about the mistake he made kissing me. I felt like it was a mistake taking a job where your boss is super hot and he will never feel the same way about you.

"Well, I hope that you enjoy your weekend Gemma," he said and got up and opened the door. "By the way, I will also be gone this weekend with some friends and you can contact me for emergencies only," he said with a wink.

"No problem," I said with a forced smile and I headed to my room.

I called my brother who agreed he could hang tonight but he was also hanging with his guys tonight. I cringed when I realized that Nate and

Will would more than likely be hanging out for guys weekend. I prayed that Will would not mention what happened in the closet. Nate and I decided it would be cool to meet up at my old job Mackey's.

I wore a pair of blue jeans that were snug and a fitted band t-shirt. I left my hair down and wore a light lip-gloss and took it easy on my eye makeup. I barely recognized myself. I was so used to hiding behind my makeup that I was starting to feel good about myself without it. I was picking up Nate so we could talk before his friends showed up. I hadn't driven in a few days and had to give a rev to the engine and she started purring in no time. I blasted the radio and spun out of the driveway. I arrived to Nate's apartment and beeped for him to bring his slow butt out.

Nate hopped in and started laughing. "You look different. Like in a good way," he said. "I take it the job is treating you well?" He asked.

"I guess," I said driving towards Mackey's. I kept the kiss with Will a secret especially, from my brother. I didn't want him to think I was some stupid little kid who can't control herself.

We chatted a little about the job and his love life until we got to the old pub. I parked the car near the entrance and locked her up with a push of a button.

I was greeted by young girls who were fresh in college just like I used to be. I ordered a beer and sat at the bar with Nate. Mackey the owner came over to me and hugged me and apologized for letting me go. He said it was a big mistake. He said I brought in the most tips. I laughed and pretended it was in the past. If he hadn't fired me I would not have landed this sweet job. I also wouldn't be tortured on a daily basis by my hot boss with split personalities.

Nate was talking on the phone while I spoke to Mackey. I turned back around and ordered another round of beers for Nate and I.

"We are going to have to get a table," he

said.

"Why?" I asked.

"My boys are coming to town and want to start early," he said.

"I will stay at the bar so, I don't mess up the testosterone at the table," I said laughing.

"Don't be stupid. You are my sister, plus I promised we would hang tonight," He said messing up my hair.

"Don't touch my hair again Nate," I said fixing my hair back in place. "Grab that table over there. I have to go to the bathroom and fix what you messed up," I said pointing towards the table by the window.

I finished fixing my hair and came out of the bathroom and I heard the infamous bell ring. That bell meant it was dance time in the bar. They played the top pop music and the girls would dance to get more tips. My old boss Mackey caught me coming out the bathroom and pointed for me to dance. I put my hands up saying no I couldn't. Then it hit me that is what the old Gemma would have done. In actuality I loved dancing and wished I had done it more.

The lights turned down and tables were moved for a make shift dance floor. I laughed and let the beat carry me and Mackey joined me. The younger girls got up on the bar and motioned their asses for money. Soon people had enough drinks to get brave and dance. The song ended and I needed to catch my breath and I ordered another drink. I turned to find my brother to see if he needed another drink. He was surrounded by a group of guys that were young and very attractive.

I thought I would do him and his buddies a favor. I nodded at the bartender. "I need a pitcher of your best beer over there at the table by the window," I said dropping a fifty to the bartender. "Oh, and send the prettiest waitress over," I said with a wink.

I made my way over to the table and all eyes met me.

I tucked my sweaty hair behind my ear. "I just told the prettiest girl over there to bring you their best beer," I said.

"I think you are the prettiest girl that could come over to this table," said a handsome friend of Nate.

"Paul, that is my sister," he said with agitation.

"Hi, I am Gemma," I said holding out my hand to shake his.

He kissed it like they do in the movies. I laughed and gave him a strange look and my eyes diverted over at Nate.

"Pleasure to meet you Gemma. Let me know if I can do anything for you," he said with a devious smile.

Nate rolled his eyes and waved me to bend down to

speak with him. "Keep your head on, douche bag is here," Nate said nodding to the bar.

The douche bag he was referring to was Ben. I rolled my eyes at the thought of him looking at me. I tried not to look over in his direction. I could feel my hands beginning to tremble. I took a big swig of beer and sat down listening to the guys talk shit. There is no way he will say anything with all these guys with me but it still felt awkward.

"Where the hell is Will?" yelled one of the guys.

"He is on his way, Greg. He of course had some business to take care of," Nate said using his fingers in quotes. They all laughed and drank. The mention of his name brought my brain back to his closet and how my body wanted him so much. The sound of them cackling broke me from my trance. The pounding thump of the bass pumping and the drums pulsating through speakers was begging me to dance.

I headed back to the floor when I heard a good song to dance to. I liked dancing by myself. I hated when guys got touchy feely on the dance floor. It was inevitable men were like magnets to women dancing. I wasn't on the floor for two minutes and Ben was standing in front of me. I tried to turn away from him and find my brother.

"Please, won't you let me explain myself to you?" he screamed over the music.

"What is there to explain?" I said still dancing and trying to ignore him.

I was feeling brave and kept moving with the music not letting him win this time. As I moved in the other direction I saw Will coming in the door. My mouth dropped opened. He looked amazing. He was wearing jeans and a dark fitted dress shirt that hugged his body. He walked over to the table where Nate and the others were chugging beers and flirting with the waitress. It was weird seeing Will socializing with people other than co-workers. My eyes moved and I noticed Paul staring at me smiling. He grabbed his glass and held it up at me acknowledging me dancing. Something about him sent chills down my spine. He was like a dirty old man in a young guy's body.

Before I knew it Ben had grabbed my arm and tried pulling me off the floor.

"Please, get your hands off me," I said nicely. Then I pointed to the table of wealthy fit men who were getting shit faced, "See those guys over there, That one with brown hair is my older brother I am pretty sure you don't want him to get riled up with all his buddies around," I said.

He released my elbow. "Please just talk to me," he pleaded.

I pointed to the bar. I took a seat and he stood close to my ear. "Gemma, I messed up and I never wanted to hurt you," he said.

"Didn't want to hurt me? You were fucking my roommate. Which, by the way she went out of her way to destroy my life a little further after that. She got me fired," I said getting angry.

My brother must have noticed and got up and was at the bar in seconds. "Is there is a problem Gemma?" he asked looking right at Ben.

"Everything is fine Nate," I sighed.

"Let me know if this guy needs to be escorted out," he said walking back to the table never breaking his sight of Ben.

"Look, I am sorry. I don't want to cause a scene or anything. I just wanted to say I was sorry in person and I miss you," he said.

I was speechless. My heart still hurt from what he did but I had also moved on. I didn't say anything back to him. I walked over to the table where the boys were hanging. They were all laughing still except Nate and Will. Nate pursed his lips together waiting for me to tell him what Ben wanted.

"Nate, I think I am going to call it an early

night," I said in his ear.

Nate shook his head no. "No you are not going to let that little prick mess up your night out. Try to enjoy yourself since your uptight boss has been working you to death," he said hitting Will in the arm.

Will just laughed and smiled. I waved at him acknowledging his presence.

"You are working for Will?" Paul shouted.

I smiled and Will just laughed. "You are one lucky son of a bitch," Paul said.

Paul definitely had a knack for making me feel uncomfortable. On a positive note, he was very attentive, never taking his eyes off me. He asked me to dance with him and I accepted. I tried not to let Ben mess up my night and danced with Paul to show him I had moved on. He was a touchy feely guy. I had to keep pushing his hands away from me.

"You are good dancer," Paul said into my ear

almost licking it.

I just smiled. "How long have you been working for Will?' he asked.

"A few weeks but, I don't want to talk about work," I said moving to the beat of the music.

I saw Nate dancing with some random girl. He kept watching Paul like a hawk. Dancing I looked over at the table where the other guys including Will were flirting with the waitress. A sense of jealously surged over me. I bit my lip and started to dance more provocatively. Paul was almost dry humping my leg and I broke for a drink back at the bar.

"Man, those guys are hot over there," said one girl to another.

I just laughed and ordered another drink. I headed back to the table. The waitress immediately got up and gave me a dirty look. "Sorry, did I just cock block you?" I asked Will?

"Something like that," he said rubbing his fingers through his hair.

"You dance pretty good," he said.

"You want to dance?" I asked Will grabbing his hands. "We are not at work so you can loosen up," I said quickly sipping my drink and holding my hand out.

"I can't," he said smiling.

"Why," I asked.

"I am not sure I can control myself when I am around you," he whispered looking into my eyes.

I wanted him right now. I wanted that kiss he gave me the other day. I kept pulling him onto the dance floor. Nate started yelling for Will. Apparently, Will had become really uptight lately and they were hoping he would loosen up.

Paul was already working on some other girl, thank God. Matter of fact they were kissing. I envied him for being so bold but I was also disgusted. I got Will out on the floor and his body began to move with mine.

"Will." I said into his ear.

"Yeah?" he said bending his head down to see me.

"You need to fire me," I said smiling.

His smile dropped, "Why?" he asked.

"I need to kiss you," I said. The drinks were working and I was being way to open. I wanted to take him back to his closet and finish what we started.

"Don't say that. Let's not mess this up," he said still dancing. It was then I realized I might have crossed that boss and employee relationship. The song finally stopped and I tried to play off what I just said to him. I went back to the table and searched for my purse and keys. My ego was bruised. I could have Ben back and have Paul but, I didn't want either of them I wanted Will. He kept rejecting me.

"Where do you think you are going? You can't drive," Will said grabbing my hands.

"I am fine," I said.

"Let me drive you back to the house," he said. It was just another quick reminder that I lived with him, as his employee.

"Fine," I said throwing my hands into the air.

"Oh, you are not leaving are you?" asked Paul. He gave me a side smile that made him look like a snake.

I shook my head yes. "Well, let me take you home," Paul insisted.

"I got this," Will chimed in. He grabbed my arm and headed out the door. "You stay here while I grab your car," he demanded.

I stood against the bricks trying not to wobble. When I dance I can totally handle the spinning but when I have to be still forget it. I closed my eyes and took a deep cleansing breath as I opened them up hoping to see my crappy Jetta with Will in it. There was the Jetta at the curb but no Will. I looked around for him when I heard a familiar voice.

"So, this is the reason why you won't talk to me?" Ben said leaning against the doorframe in front of Mackey's

I rolled my eyes trying to ignore him.

"I should have known better than to fall for someone like you," he said.

"What?' my voice shook. My hands began to shake and I was sobering up quick. I felt a touch on my elbow and Will was standing next to me. Will's jaw clenched and he balled his hand into a fist.

"Let's go Gemma," Will hissed.

"You were always too good for everybody. I see a guy has to have money to get you in bed," he said with a smirk.

"Fuck You Ben," I yelled.

"If we had I wouldn't have been fucking your roommate," he yelled loud enough to humiliate me in front of everyone.

Before I could move Will had punched Ben in the face. Will quickly pulled me into my car and drove away.

Chapter 5

Just a little fun

I had never wanted Will to see me inebriated or humiliated by my ex boyfriend. I couldn't believe Ben thought he could win me back then just trash me all over again. I guess things never do change. It occurred to me that Julie must have dumped him if he wanted to get back with me so soon. In a way I felt sorry for him because, Will punched him pretty hard and I rejected him this time. I didn't say anything as I waited in the car for Will to leave. I stared out the window-watching people gathering around Ben trying to help him to his feet. Will mumbled a few unclear words and pulled away. My neck craned watching people drag him back into the bar. I know if it had been Nate outside he would have done the same thing or worse. The ride home was silent until Will's phone chimed breaking the hum in my ears.

"Yeah," he said to a voice on the phone.

"Well, that son of a bitch got out of line with Gemma and so I decked him," he said. Knowing Nate he was probably furious. "Yeah, she is right here. Hold on," he said handing me his phone.

"Hello?" I said. My hands were shaking and I swallowed hard not cry.

"What the hell happened, Gemma?" Nate asked.

A lump in my throat grew and my eyes stung with tears. "He said I thought I was too good for him and the reason I wouldn't sleep with him was because he didn't have money," I said choking back tears.

"Hmmm. Then Will punched him?" Nate asked.

"Yep," I said.

Laughter broke out on the other side of the phone. "Gemma, Ben got what he deserved and he is lucky I wasn't out there," Nate said.

"Let me talk to Will please," he said.

I handed the phone back to Will. I turned my head and stared out the window. The last couple of days had been confusing and emotionally draining. Everything I had to drink was wearing off and my head started to hurt. Will pulled up to his long driveway and parked my sad looking car on the side of the house. He cut the engine and touched my chin gently.

"Gemma, are you okay?" he asked.

"Yeah, Ben is just a jerk and I wish I could have hit him myself," I said pulling away from him.

Will let out a chuckle and got out of the car

fast enough to open my door. Charles opened the door and greeted us. He gave us a concerned look like a father that knew we were up to no good. Will guided me with the palm of his hand on my back towards the kitchen.

"Is everything ok sir," asked Charles.

"Yeah Charles, we just ran into some trouble but everything is fine now. You can go to bed," Will said. He kept his eyes on me the whole time.

Will got us both bottled water and insisted that I drink as much water as I could. My eyes felt like sandbags the bottle of water felt like a ten-pound weight in hands. I laid my head on my arms that fell on the table. The next thing I remember was Will carrying me up the stairs.

He opened my bedroom door careful not to hit my head or legs on the door. He laid my back onto the purple bed. He sat on the edge of the bed and moved my loose hairs away from my face. I smiled when his fingers brushed my face. I peeked through the tired slits of my eyes. I had often fantasized about being in his arms and I was saddened as he got up. He didn't leave yet; instead he took my shoes off and pulled the covers over me.

"Don't go," I whispered out.

"Gemma," he said.

"Just stay here until I fall asleep, "I said grabbing his hand and cupping my face.

He sat on the bed and combed my hair with his fingers sending chills over my skin.

"You warm enough?" Will asked in a hushed voice.

"Yeah, Why?" I said.

"You have goose bumps all over," He said rubbing my arms.

"It's you," I said cracking a small smile.

He puffed a laugh out loud and moved in closer to me lending his body heat to me.

"Can I ask you something Gemma?" Will said.

"Yeah," I said keeping my eyes closed and enjoying his body next to me.

"What happened with you and Ben? Why did he say those things about you?" he said. His body tensed up and stopped touching my hair.

I pulled myself up onto my elbows. "Well, Ben and I were dating but we never had sex. I kept busy in college and work. We had some attraction and when I thought I was ready to go further with him he started to change. One night Mackey's was slow and they let me go home early. When I got home I saw Ben and my roommate Julie fucking on the floor," I said holding back my tears. I hadn't told anybody else but Nate and I couldn't really tell him everything.

"I am glad I punched him more so now," he said

I looked at him and smiled. "I am kind of jealous because, I kind of wanted to take a punch at him," I said.

"All right, my turn to ask you a question," I said.

"Hurry up, I have to get ready for my boy weekend," he said.

"Will you fire me?" I asked.

"Gemma, you are a strange girl. Why do you insist that I fire you tonight?" he said cocking his head to the side.

"So I won't feel bad," I said.

"Feel bad for what?" Will asked.

"For this," I said pulling myself closer to him. I placed my lips over his and he pushed his tongue into my mouth. I pulled him closer to me and sat on my knees in front of him. His kiss sent waves of electricity throughout my body. He didn't refuse me or push me away. I un-tucked his shirt from his pants and ran my hands over his chest tugging his shirt. He slowly raised my t-shirt off me.

"Gemma, You sure you want to do this, now?" he asked. He sat in my bedroom shirtless revealing his super model body.

I said nothing and continued to kiss him everywhere on his chest. He let out low groans that rumbled from his chest. I almost had his pants undone when there was a small knock at my bedroom door. We both stopped and looked at each other like our parents caught us.

"Yeah," I said holding still.

"Excuse me but, Master Will you have a visitor here," Charlotte said.

"I will be right there," he said letting out a sigh. He rubbed his face with hands and grabbed his shirt off the floor.

I fell back onto the bed still in my bra feeling frustrated. I turned away from the door as he left my bedroom. I was starting to think that something was trying to keep us apart. After a few moments there was another tap at the door except it was Will.

"Get dressed, the cops are here and want to ask about what happened tonight with Ben," he said with his jaw clenching.

I grabbed my shirt that was hanging on the edge of the bed and scuffled downstairs. The officers were rude and blunt. I explained that Ben was a drunken disgruntled ex-boyfriend and he got out of line. I admitted Will punched him in my defense for being rude. The cops said sorry Ben was pressing charges and Will was handcuffed and sent to jail for the night. My chest ached with guilt seeing him hauled off into a police car.

"I will pick you up as soon as possible," I said to Will.

I cried myself to sleep that night knowing this was my entire fault.

Chapter 6

Fired and Rehired

Charlotte woke me up by seven and made me a cup of tea. I called the jail and asked what time Will would be released. They told me he would be released around ten. I showered and drove my trusty little Jetta to the county police station. Trying to make up for what happened I brought Will a cup of coffee that I held in my hand. An older police officer escorted Will out. He was wearing the outfit that I was tearing off him last night. He looked like hell. His hair was disheveled and his eyes had circles around them. He said nothing to me as I paid his bail with his credit card. I drove us back to his house. He was silent the whole way back to his house not answering his phone that was going off every couple minutes.

Once back home Will headed right for the stairs to his room still not speaking to me. Charles the butler came down shortly with bags from Will's room.

His driver was waiting out front for him. He was still going away for his boy's weekend. I watched Will walk down the stairs and talk to Charlotte and Charles. He didn't speak to me or even look at me.

"Have fun," I said waving. He kept walking. We were back to his split personality. I get that he was mad at me. I never made him punch my ex. He took it upon himself. He was angry with me and now I was getting the cold shoulder. The day went by and I tried to enjoy it. I stayed around the house.

I read out by the garden and even had lunch with Charlotte there.

"Charlotte, Is that the guest house?" I asked pointing to a small house by the pool.

"Yeah, it is also the pool house," she said.

"Is it occupied?" I asked.

"No, it is rarely used anymore," she said.

"Do you think Charles could help me move into it this weekend?" I asked.

"Master Campbell, will be upset but, I think Charles would help you," she said creasing her brows.

I spent the rest of the afternoon moving my things to the pool house. I figured he was giving me the cold shoulder because he wanted to distance himself from me. The pool house was perfect. It had its own kitchen and my own office beside the bedroom. *Why hadn't he placed me here in the beginning?* The only thing I was missing was my purple bedding I loved so much. I could always buy one if I wanted. Sunday rolled around and I was deflated. I spent time swimming laps in my boss's pool. I lay by the pool in a bikini that I had purchased two summers ago. I put my ear buds in and covered my eyes with my huge sunglasses. My eyes were shut and I was starting to drift asleep when I felt a cool finger brush my shoulder. I ripped the ear buds out of my ears by the cord, which sent a pain into my head. It was Paul.

"Hey there Gemma, Does your boss know you are slacking on the job?" he said violating me with his eyes.

"I am off this weekend and he is supposed to be doing his guys weekend thing," I said covering myself up with a towel.

"Will left early for some business thing but I need to speak with him and he isn't taking my calls," he said pulling up a chair next to me.

"Well, leave him a voicemail," I said.

Paul’s skin was flawless like Will’s but Paul was rude and didn’t treat women right. Paul also carried a creepy vibe within his good looks. He may be good looking but he was only after a few things. He wanted women and Will’s life. He covered his eyes with his hands against the scorching sun.

“Will left yesterday and I haven’t heard anything from him,” I said.

“Could you have him call me when he gets back?” he asked.

I shook my head yes and waited for him to walk away.

“By the way, you look fantastic in a bikini,” he said with a wink and walked away.

Vomit entered my mouth. Why does he have to be foul? I wanted nothing more than to spend the rest of my day by the pool but work was already coming in through email.

I placed a sarong around my waist and went to

my new office and home. I forwarded emails for meetings to Will including a text message about Paul.

It was only a few hours later my door crashed open. I flew out of my chair and grabbed my chest.

"What the hell do you think you are doing Gemma?" Will yelled. His body was tense and his mouth was tight.

"You weren't talking to me and I felt bad about everything. I thought if I gave us some distance that it would make our business relationship better," I said playing with the tie on my sarong.

"You are driving me mad Gemma," he said shaking his head.

"Me? What about you Jekyll and Hyde? One minute you are a hard ass boss then you are all over me. What is it you want from me?" I yelled back at him.

"Look I have a job to do and I have to keep what I can secret but, it is hard with you," he said.

"Maybe I should get another job and get out of your life then," I choked out. Those words hurt to even say. I wanted to be in his bed as his one and only but, he wouldn't let me in his life. He kept pushing me away or by some force of nature we were being kept apart.

"I don't want you to leave but, if you need to live in the pool house so be it but, you can't ever wear that again," he said pointing to my outfit.

"What?" I asked looking down at my body. I realized I was standing in my bikini with only a sarong around my waist.

I desired him more knowing he didn't want me to leave but respected I needed my space. I could see the hunger in his eyes. I felt it too and I got a surge of bravery.

"Oh, you don't want me to wear me this? Okay,"

I said removing my sarong.

"No, Gemma I was talking about your bikini. You can't walk around in that especially if Paul is around," he said rolling his eyes.

"I can't wear my bikini, huh?" I said undoing the strings of my top.

"Guess what Paul isn't here," I said dropping my bottoms to the floor.

Will closed the door behind him and picked me up and carried me to the bedroom. His body was still tense.

"Gemma, You are fired," he said laying me on the bed. He tore his clothes from his body and lay on top of me kissing me passionately. I groaned into his mouth with each kiss getting deeper. I stared into his eyes as he pushed himself inside me. I rubbed my fingertips down his back onto his buttocks. I cupped him pushing him deeper inside me. My body quivered as he moved faster and my breathing stayed a steady pace. An explosion released in my body and I moaned into his ear. I called his name just like I had fantasized about. He then tensed up as he climaxed and his body collapsed on top of mine. He kissed my head and gently moved to my side never letting go of me but with his legs wrapped around mine.

Staring into his eyes I said, "Will, on what grounds am I fired?"

He smiled and said, "Sexual harassment against your boss."

I laughed smoothing his hair away from his face. He was absolutely beautiful. He smiled showing a toothy grin.

"Maybe, I should take it up with human resources?" I said with a smirk.

"Maybe," he said.

"You smell like sweet candy," he said as he nuzzled my neck.

His lips swept over my neck and I was ready

for him again but a buzz from his phone broke our meeting.

He peeked at the caller id. "Jesus, It's Paul. Relentless ass," he said pushing himself up on the bed.

My shoulders dropped as he took the call from Mr. Creepy. I wanted to finish what we started so, I thought I would distract him. I started kissing him on his neck then proceeded my way down. His voice cracked, as I got closer to his crotch.

"Paul, I am in the middle of a meeting, can I call you later?" he said as he grasped my hair with his hands pushing him into my mouth. He threw his phone on the nightstand as I made myself more comfortable with his manhood.

His body tensed and he let out a loud cry for me. He lay still on my bed in euphoria I studied his body. I used my index finger to trace the ripples of muscles.

"Gemma, You are rehired. Matter of fact we

have lots of work to get done today. Plus, tonight we have a charity event to get to," he said.

"Tonight, I didn't get word about an event for tonight. Plus, I am off this weekend," I said creasing my brow.

"Well, you were busy in a meeting but, Paul so kindly reminded me about bringing somebody to this event," he said rolling his eyes.

"What? Why are you rolling your eyes?" I asked.

"Paul wanted to know if he could take you to this charity ball tonight?" he said.

"Ugh, that guy is so creepy. You didn't say yes did you?" I said propping myself onto his chest.

"I didn't get time to answer because I was interrupted. I wanted you to go with me," he said touching my chin.

"I would love to go with you but," my voice

cracked.

"What?" he asked.

"Never mind, let's not spoil a good moment," I said wrapping up in my blanket.

"I will pay you for time and half for tonight if you like," he said.

"You make me feel like some whore when you say that," I said in a low voice.

"I didn't mean that I was just worried since it was supposed to be your day off," he said wrapping his arms around my waist.

"Can I ask you something?" I said.

"Yeah," he said,

"How is this going to work?" I asked. The words were hard to press out of my mouth. I expected the worse and hoped for the best. I wanted nothing more than to be with Will exclusively. "I mean I know you are seeing Liza and whoever else you see," I said biting the inside of my cheek.

Will let out a small sigh. "Gemma, I am completely smitten with you. You are incredibly smart and beautiful. Plus, you put up with my mood swings and creepy friends," he said looking at me with his deep blue eyes. "I still want you to work for me if that is what you are asking but, I want you to feel okay with it," he said.

"I need the job but, I want to be the only woman in your life," I said. My voice cracked again. I didn't regret my request.

"Do you realize I went to jail over the weekend for hitting your ex-boyfriend?" he said.

"Ben deserved it but, if you didn't hit him I would have," I said.

He pressed his lips again mine. They were like warm silk brushing my lips. I was getting lost in the moment again.

"Gemma, we will never get anything done if we

keep going," He said looking for his pants. "When I get back to the main house I will ask Charles to help you move back in,"

"I don't want to," I said under my breath.

"You don't?" he asked. His face dropped and I felt guilty for it. "Why?"

"I think it is nice having a little space from my boss and my lover," I said. I kissed his face like it was his bruised ego. He wrapped his hands around my waist and picked me up off the bed.

"If that is what you want then I will do it but, you will have to spend the night with me sometime," he said. My mind went back to the first kiss in his closet when he asked me to help him with his tie.

"Go shower and get ready," he said finishing getting dressed.

He left me to the pool house at my request and I didn't feel weird about it. It made me feel on my own. He was an amazing man and great in bed. Not that I had much to compare it to. I had only slept with one other guy and that was my first year of college and it sucked. It was the worst and most uncomfortable experience ever. I vowed I wouldn't sleep with a guy again until I felt absolutely certain that I was ready. The scary thing was I wanted to sleep with Will since I interviewed for the job.

Chapter 7

Who am I?

My skin was bronzed from lying in the sun earlier. It made my hair look lighter. I stepped into the silky purple dress. The dress made me feel like a movie star. I usually pulled my hair back tight for work but since this was a dressy event I wanted to look amazing. I pinned just one side of my hair with a butterfly hairpiece that was small and encrusted with tiny jewels. The rest of my hair rested on my shoulders in curls. I swept some translucent powder over my face highlighting my cheeks with blush. I kept my makeup light with emphasis on my eyes. My eyes had a tint of purple that reflected from my dress. I felt like I was going to prom. I had never been this dressed up since then. At least, I knew my date for the evening was super hot and I might get a good night kiss.

Will knocked on the door to the pool house where I decided to stay against his wishes. I opened the door. Will was dressed in a tux except he didn't have a tie on.

"I need some help with my bow tie and I know how good you are with ties," he said with a side smile.

I laughed and stretched on my tiptoes to finish getting him ready.

"You look beautiful Gemma," he said brushing his knuckles along my cheekbone.

"You don't look so bad yourself," I said

putting the finishing touches on his bow tie.

He placed his lips on mine slow and soft careful not to mess up my face and get makeup on him.

I grabbed my silver heels pulling my dress up revealing my tanned legs.

"Let's get this over with before I explode," He said. He grabbed me and kissed me harder and his manhood dug into my waist.

My head spun as he released me from his tight hold. My body tingled, as it wanted nothing more to have his lips on me. I let out a moan and he kissed my neck.

Will smiled, "We should go James has been waiting for twenty minutes," he said licking his lips. I checked myself one last time in the mirror fixing the loose hairs and touching up my face. I sprayed my wrists and neck with my favorite perfume.

I had no idea what to expect from the charity event. My stomach began to ache when we entered the car.

"You ok?" Will asked.

"I am kind of nervous. I don't know what to expect or who anybody is?" I said chewing the inside of my mouth.

"Well, I will introduce you to everybody. Paul will be there of course but, the way you look tonight I ask you to stay away from him," He said touching my knee.

"I didn't get a chance to check out what the charity was for," I said.

"It's to bring awareness to starving children and to end child hunger," he said.

"I have one more question," I said. My voice shook and I played with the hem of my dress.

"What? Why are you so nervous to ask me?" he said pulling my chin up.

"How will you introduce me?" I asked. My body tensed as the words left my mouth. Of course I didn't want him to call me his lover but what exactly were we?

His lips parted and he licked them staying cool when he answered, "I will introduce you as my date," he said moving his hand up my thigh.

"Paul knows I am your assistant. He will know I am not your date," I said.

"Who cares about Paul? You are mine and that is all that matters. Let's work out the rest of the technicalities later. I am happy to have you still work for me but, I want to be more than just your boss," he said.

His words made my heart flutter. I had an endless smile for the whole night. We arrived at a hotel ballroom that was filled with ice sculptures and elaborate decorations. The lighting was very dim and they played older music. Will looped his arm through mine and guided me to more people to meet. I was handling everything well until Paul came over.

"My Gemma, you look amazing tonight," he said in his usual creepy way.

I could sense a bit of jealously as he looked over to Will. Paul was good looking in his own way but his attitude and arrogance made him unattractive. He leaned into Will and whispered something in his ear. I watched Will and his jaw tightened and he gripped my arm tighter.

Will cleared his throat, "I don't think that is any of your concern Paul," he said.

Paul dusted his tuxedo sleeve and said, "Gemma, please make sure you save me a dance tonight. I got to find my date," waving at some dark haired woman by the bar.

"What did he say that pissed you off that bad?" I asked out the side of mouth keeping a smile as we walked past people.

"Trust me you don't want to know," he said and guided me to the dance floor.

"I probably don't but why is he like that?" I asked holding his shoulder with one hand and his hand with the other.

"I met Paul in college with your brother. He can be a great guy at times but, most of the time he is a sneaky son of a bitch," he said. I stared into his eyes and wondered what he was thinking.

"See it isn't so bad is it?" as he spun me around.

I let out a little giggle. "I am having a good time but, that is only because I am here with you," I said.

"Do you mind if I cut in?" Paul asked.

"That is up to the Gemma," Will said looking at me.

I couldn't refuse Paul in front of all these people.

"Sure, but my feet are starting to hurt," I said.

"I will get us some drinks and get us a table," Will said with a sorry face.

Paul placed his hand tight around my waist pulling me close to him. He smelled of alcohol and cologne.

"Where is your date?" I asked trying to loosen his grip.

"Ahhh, she is over there flirting with your boss. Or should I say date?" he said pointing to the bar.

"Will is one lucky man," he said.

"Why is that?" I asked. I should have known better to ask that because of whom I was dealing with.

"Well, he has a great job that he keeps from his friends and he gets to fuck the help," he said.

My hand stung as I slapped him across the face

and pushed him away from me. I stormed off the dance floor fighting back tears. I searched for the nearest ladies room. I refused to let that jerk ruin my night. Thankfully, nobody was in there and I dabbed my eyes so my makeup wouldn't run. I washed my hands before leaving when Paul's date came in. She was staggering to find the bathroom. We exchanged looks and she gave me a fake plastered smile.

She held onto the stall door and said, "Girl, I would pay good money to have your date tonight," she said as her ankle slid out of from her shoe. She caught herself with both hands on the door. I figured she had to be drunk to be with Paul.

I walked to open the door and she mumbled out," Don't think you are better than me. He had many assistants before you," she said slamming the stall door.

The night was getting worse by the minute. I wanted to be back at Will's pool house with him in my bed loving me. I knew that Paul and the drunken date of his were right. I am nobody special and he was just fucking me. I walked slowly to the tables and found Will standing and giving me a wave.

Will pulled me closer to him with his one arm by the shoulder. My body immediately became rigid. I felt dirty and worthless.

"What's the matter Gemma?" he asked. His forehead creased with concern. He rubbed my arms like he was warming me up. He pulled the chair out for me gently tucking the seat underneath me.

I leaned in and whispered in his ear, "I am just not feeling so well," I lied. How many other girls had he brought to one of these events? I mean he just brought Liza last week. I was the flavor of the week and now Paul knew I was now having an affair with Will. Paul's date said it clearly and I knew I was nothing special. She may be completely shit faced but she was right.

"We can leave after the speech and get you back home," he said. He moved his chair in closer to mine putting his arm around the back of my chair. I slid myself to the edge of my chair leaning forward trying to avoid his touch. Every moment I felt sicker. Questions filled my fuzzy head. How many other assistants has he had? Why do I have to work at his house? Why not his office? What exactly is he hiding from everyone? I guzzled the champagne in front of me. Will remained silent the rest of the evening and I stayed distant. His mouth stayed tight and he shook his foot underneath the table. He squeezed his knuckles every time he saw Paul.

The night dragged and finally we were back in the car with James. My night suddenly got more awkward. I stared out the window avoiding him. I leaned my chin on my hand and watched the passing cars like I would do when I was a child.

"Did I do something to offend you tonight?" he asked.

I couldn't find the words to talk. I swallowed hard fighting back my tears of embarrassment. He grabbed my hand and placed it in his. His hands were warm and overlapped mine.

"Please Gemma talk to me," he said pulling my chin to look at him.

"I just don't know how this is going to work. I am not like Liza and I am getting over this really awful relationship. What makes matters worse is that you are my boss," I said pushing my hair behind my ear.

"Please don't worry about how this will work. You can live at the pool house if you need space. If you want time off just let me know. As far as your past relationship, we can take things slow. I didn't mean to overwhelm you with tonight but, think of it as a work thing if that helps," he said with a little smile.

"Can I ask you something?" I said shifting my body towards him.

Will shook his head. "What did Paul say to you

tonight that upset you so much?"

He pursed his lips and exhaled loudly. "It isn't important. What happened in the bathroom?" he said challenging me.

I hesitated for a moment and I decided maybe I should just be honest. "Well, Paul's drunk date told me I was not special," I said looking down at the floor.

"So you listened to her? " He asked with irritation in his voice.

"No, she said other stuff too," I said rolling my eyes

"Well, come out with it. The sooner you are honest with me the sooner we will be able to get past it," Will said rubbing his finger over my knuckles.

I let out a deep breath trying to find my courage to be honest. "She said I was just like the other assistants and I was not any better than she was," I said trying to hold my tears back.

Will let go of my hand and shifted himself in the seat. He didn't say anything to me and that scared me. He just confirmed that I was just another assistant that he was having casual sex with.

"So, that is it? You are not going to say anything?" I asked. I was feeling angry. Maybe I should go to a shrink and talk about why I am always putting myself in theses stupid situations. Maybe I was careless and or blind. Maybe I was just naïve for thinking someone would actually want to spend time with me and like me for me. I was a smart girl when it came to book smarts but as far as men I was still in the bottom of my class.

Will ignored me for the rest of the night. He got out of the car without looking at me. He still held the door for me but wouldn't dare touch me. The next few days were filled with coldness in the air. I retreated to the pool house and worked in silence in my office and avoided him. I found myself barely sleeping. It is hard to get over someone when you work and live with them.

A few days later I got a knock at the door. Will was there pacing the doorway. He looked different like he was tired.

"What can I help you with Mr. Campbell?" I said through the crack of the door.

"So we are back to being formal?" Will said. Before I could answer he interrupted, "Look I didn't come over to fight. I came to tell you that….I care for you more than I have cared for someone ever. It hurt that you would take anything serious from that drunken woman that Paul brought," he said. His body flexed when he spoke to me.

"How many other girls or assistants have you brought? Is that why I stay at your house so I see nobody else but you?" I said suspiciously.

"Don't insult me Gemma. I don't have to hire a woman to work for me to sleep with them," he said clenching his jaw. I knew by his tone I was pissing him off.

"Why me then? What is so special about me?" I asked.

"You honestly don't see yourself well do you? Do you even remember meeting me when your brother came home from college for break?" he said.

I rewound my thoughts to that time. My long-term memory had been on halt since my recent life had been hectic. I shook my head no.

"You honestly don't remember do you? It was Christmas break and you were still in high school. Nate brought a couple of us by and you were helping your mother make cookies. I saw you and I knew you were the most beautiful thing I had ever seen. I knew I wanted to be with you. I watched you. The way you moved and how you smiled," he said pulling me close to him.

My heart did back flips. I remembered Nate bringing in loud friends and they all being older than me. Of course I thought they were cute. I was just a high school girl and they were more experienced in life. My mother spoke to them while I baked the cookies. Then it dawned on me. Will was the only one to say thank you for the cookies.

As much as I wanted this to be true he still had affairs with his employees and dated loud women. "If that is true what about the other assistants and Liza?" I asked staring at the floor kicking it.

He picked my chin up and looked into my eyes. "Gemma Carter, I only had one other relationship with an assistant and she quit. Liza is my old college girlfriend. She seems to weasel herself back to me when she has nothing going on," he said. He kissed my lips but I pulled away wanting more answers.

"Why do you sleep with Liza if you don't care for her?" I asked.

"I have needs Gemma and you working with me was driving me crazy. I didn't want to push since you just started working for me and make it all weird," he said.

"You don't think it is weird now?" I interrupted with a laugh.

"No it is weird but I feel less stressed when I am with you. I feel very at ease but, there is one problem," he said.

"What?" I asked.

"I need you stay away from Paul. He has some hidden agenda to get you in his bed and I can't have that," he said rubbing his fingers through my hair. "One more thing, are you ever going to invite me in?" he said with a toothy smile.

"Please come in," I said waving my hand inside the house. He sat on the couch crossing his legs. He placed his arm on the back of the couch. "You like it here in the pool house?" he asked looking around.

"Yeah, It is kind of what I need. You seem to

be a bit spoiled with all the help," I said sitting next to him.

"Sorry, if I have been cold to you but, you confuse me sometimes and I don't like the fact you would take Paul's date as a reliable source," he said.

"You are forgiven. However, I will need a raise, "I said raising my brows.

"Is that so?" he asked with a smirk. "What kind of raise Ms. Carter?"

"I will need you to kiss me here," I said pointing my finger to my lips.

"That can be arranged anything else?" he said as he leaned and kissed my lower lip.

"Here," I pointed to my underneath my ear. He moved his tongue down and nibbled on my neck. Chills exploded from my skin and my body ached for more kisses. I leaned back on the couch arching my back. He began kissing my collarbone cupping my breast. My body was aching and I kept my fingers in his hair guiding him. He ran his hand underneath my shirt rubbing my breast over my bra. He kissed my stomach and I giggled. His scruffy hair on his chin tickled me with every kiss. He moved his hands back up to my breast placing them out of the cup of my bra. His warm mouth touched my nipples and loud moans escaped me.

"You are driving me crazy," I said breathy. He looked up and smiled continuing using his mouth as a weapon against my body.

I couldn't take anymore and I frantically began to take his shirt off and unbutton his slacks. It didn't take long before he was naked on top of me on the couch. My body grew more impatient for him to be inside me. I pushed my hips toward him signaling I wanted him now. He got the message and proceeded. I relaxed my thighs as he slid in deeper. I let out a loud exhale and his hair hung loosely in his face. I brushed it back with my fingers so I could see his blue eyes. He was the most beautiful man I have been with. His body was like a god and he was with me. Each thrust from his hips sent me into ecstasy. We picked up our rhythm and I began to pant with joy. I could feel my breathing stop as I concentrated and exploded with joy and pleasure screaming his name out loud. He in return picked up his pace and let out a moan and a long breath of air.

We lay on the couch forgetting about the other night. His eyes closed from exhaustion and I lay looking at him. My brain did ponder if we were just friends with benefits or an actual couple. I didn't dare ask. I was afraid to ruin the moment. He smiled when he opened his eyes and saw me staring at him.

"Is your raise sufficient?" He asked with a devilish smile.

I smiled and laughed. "Yes, but my guy won't like me sleeping with my boss," I said jokingly.

"Who is your guy?" he asked raising his brow.

"You are," I said kissing his warm lips.

"I was worried there for a minute," he said kissing me back.

"I do have to tell you that I have a meeting to go to downtown so, I should get ready. Would you like to have dinner with me tonight in the main house?" he asked.

"That sounds great," I said.

Time crept as he attended some boring meeting and I wrapped up a few travel arrangements and sent out birthday cards. It was then it struck me that my mom's birthday was coming up and I should think about visiting her.

I reminded my brother that our mother's birthday was coming up and we should visit her and take her out. I got a text from my brother saying that he would try to make it down to Williamsburg, Virginia to see mom when he could. I was kind of hoping that we could ride together but I would make the most of it. I hadn't spoken to my mother much since I graduated college. Mostly, because I felt ashamed that I was not doing as great as my friends and brother were. She has changed since my father left her. He waited until Nate and I were adults to finally leave my mother. His excuse of not being in love with her anymore was lame and unexpected and she continuously blames herself. I don't think people fall out of love. I think they just give up on love. They get tired of trying or don't want to work at it. After thinking hard about my mom and her situation I was beginning to think it was a curse, maybe it only affects on the women.

We visited my mom at our childhood home. It still was decorated the same. My mom never took down any family photos. She didn't want to let go of any memories. I had a blast hanging with my mom and brother looking at old photo albums. It was just what I needed. I needed a break from Will's split personality and my computer. Will didn't email, call, or even text me. A part of me felt bad for wishing he had. Mom called it an early night and went to bed. Nate waited for mom close the door and he called me outside on the front porch. Nate took it upon his self to give me a heart to heart.

"Gemma, I am not sure what is going on with you and Will but, don't mess up your life for him," he said. I appreciated him being a big brother but he was getting into my personal life now.

"Nate, my job is fine and please stay out of my personal life," I said trying to avoid the subject.

"Look, Paul told me that you and Will are more than co-workers," he said.

"Well, first of all Paul is a creepy asshole and you should not always listen to him. Second of all what happens to me in my personal life is not Paul's or your business," I said as I stormed off.

"I just don't want to see you get your hopes up," he yelled at me.

What the hell did he mean he didn't want me to get my hopes up? I am pretty sure that was my second warning from an outsider. Why would Nate even listen to Paul? Paul has been trying to get in my pants since he met me at Mackey's.

I stomped my way back to my old room. I flopped on my bed as I fumed about everybody sticking their nose into my business. I pulled my phone out and checked for messages. Still nothing from Will and my heart grew scared and anxious. I toyed with calling him or texting him. I refrained myself from being too desperate and needy.

The next day we had a big meal outside at an Italian restaurant. My mom started to talk about how things were going for both of us. Nate of course bragged that he was doing great but hadn't found a lucky lady to call his wife. He felt like he needed to look some more. My mom smiled and looked at me.

"What about you Gemma? How is everything?" she asked with a bit of sadness in her eyes.

Both Nate and I looked at each other. "Well, I had a few bumps in the road but, I found a great job and possibly a guy," I said. My face warmed and my chest felt like it was in vice.

My mom grabbed my hand and said, "I am so glad you both took the time from your busy lives to come down to see me," she said. Tears welled up in her eyes.

"I never thought I would be in my fifties single and lonely. I pray that you both will find love and grow old with that person," she said as tears spilled down her cheeks.

"Mom, stop you are supposed to be having fun on your birthday," I said handing her a napkin.

The weekend left me feeling a bit sad and I couldn't wait to see Will again. I needed to discuss where this relationship was going. If he has cared for me this long then taking it to another level shouldn't be a problem. I pulled into the long driveway and saw a nice silver sports car in the driveway.

Chapter 8

Weekend

I drove past where the help parks their cars. I squinted to see if I could see anyone in the house. Charlotte came outside to dump the kitchen trash. I waved to her acknowledging that she was important to me and that I had missed her. She walked up slowly to me flattening out her apron.

"Ms. Carter," she said. Her face fell like she had something to tell me. By the look on her face it was bad.

"Charlotte, call me Gemma," I said with a smile.

"Gemma, I am not sure how to say this," she said clasping her hands together.

"Out with it Charlotte," I demanded.

"Master Campbell is with someone and doesn't want to be disturbed," she said as she flinched.

"Ok, like a business meeting?" I asked.

She shook her head no. "I am assuming at this point that he is not with a man right now. You are trying to stall me because he is in the house with another woman?" I asked. My face was feeling hot.

I could feel pulse racing throughout my body. *That son of a bitch. What do I do? I did what any normal girl would have done.* I needed to check for myself. I walked past Charlotte towards the side kitchen entrance.

"Gemma, don't," she said holding me by the arm. I pulled away from her and ran to the house to the kitchen entrance.

I tiptoed into the kitchen. There was not much sound coming from the lower level so, I proceeded upstairs. I followed the hushed voices near my old room. Oh my god! He has some woman in my old bedroom. I tried to peek but I couldn't bring myself to it. I knew it was him by his deep smooth voice when he spoke in a low tone. I knew his voice anywhere.

I ran down the steps nearly tripping over my own feet. Tears erupted from face. I ran to the pool house. *How could I have been such a fool to fall for my boss and think I was his one and only love interest? I am stuck in the same fucking cycle.* I cried most of the night until I fell asleep. Charlotte came over a few times to make sure I was eating.

That night after everything was quiet I decided to write a letter. It would be my resignation letter. I hesitated as I signed my name and sealed the envelope. The next morning I was to be in the main house by eight am sharp. I pulled my hair back into a tight ponytail and let my bangs swoop to the side. I pulled on my slacks and white blouse I interviewed in.

I grabbed a cup of tea from the kitchen and headed towards my office not making note of Will's presence. I emailed the latest information regarding his meetings for the next two weeks. I kept the letter tucked inside of my purse. I tried to think of the best time to speak to him in person about me leaving. He stood his distance as well as if he knew that he had done wrong. I was in the middle of looking for another job when Will walked into the room. I quickly closed the window on my browser careful for him not to see it.

"Did you and Nate have a good time this weekend?" he asked.

I opened my email back up looking like I was hard at work. "Uh yeah, we had a good time," I said not looking up at him but for a second.

"When did you get home?" he asked.

"Um, sometime earlier on Saturday," I said chewing my lip.

"Hmm," he said as he walked away.

I pulled my browser back open and searched again for jobs. I wasn't going to be left high and dry again. I am not going to be the victim of some man. I wrote down a few emails to send my resume to and closed the browser. I tiptoed back to the pool house careful for Will not to see me.

I asked Charlotte to find me boxes so that I could start packing. They were waiting for me when I arrived in the pool house. There was also one thing waiting for me in the pool house. Will was sitting on my couch with my letter of resignation.

"So this is what you do? When things don't work your way you run?" he asked waving the letter.

"How did you get that?" I asked. I could have sworn I had stuffed that letter deep in my purse.

"It was on the floor in your office today. Do you mind telling me what is wrong and where you are going?" He asked shaking the letter.

"I heard you on Saturday. I heard you with another woman in my old room," I choked out.

"Oh, this explains the cold shoulder and no lunch breaks," he said. "Well, before you just pick up and leave. Why don't go look at the room," he said. "No go on Gemma."

"Why would I want to see the place where you fornicated with some woman?" I asked. *What the hell was he thinking?* Please rub it in my face some more. Will is a god and I am some mediocre girl.

"I did not fornicate with some woman. I was having your room redone to try and get you back into the main house," he said getting up from the couch.

I kicked my foot at the corner of the desk. I couldn't bear to look him in the eyes. I was such a fool not to trust him. He picked my chin up with his hand.

"Hey, I told you I have been waiting for you. I finally get you and you run. Please let me show you what I am doing to the room," he said gently rubbing my back.

"Why did Charlotte tell me you were with another woman?" I asked confused.

"Well, technically she was right but she was misinformed. Please let me show you." He said guiding me with his hand behind my back.

"You are having trust issues based on your recent relationship or have you been for a while?" He asked. Was he my shrink or lover? I did start to ponder his question. I walked in silence back to the main house. My body longed for more of his touch. It was like he had electricity in his fingers. I contemplated that Ben and Julie had ruined me from loving and trusting again. To think about it my mom and dad are now divorced after forty years of marriage. It seemed like love was too easy to walk away from. When things go bad you leave or hurt the other person sometimes, both.

"Are you going to talk to me?" he asked. I smiled feeling foolish for accusing him of cheating on me while he was trying to do something nice for me.

"Yes," I whispered.

We walked up the stairs and he led me to my old room. He stopped in front of the door turning to look at me. "Gemma, this is my way of making you feel more comfortable here. I want you to move back here," he said. He turned the knob behind his back and pushed opened the door.

White covers and blue prints lie on the bed. He arranged to extend my room to take over the entire wing. He picked colors that would complement the purple I love so much. "See, I didn't fornicate with anyone here," he said. "But, if you want to I can arrange that," he said with a coy smile.

"Hmmm. I heard make up sex is great but I

guess we would have to break up to make up. Since, we are not a couple I guess it is just casual sex," I said leaning into him nipping his lower lip with my teeth.

"Are you asking me to be your boyfriend Ms. Carter?" he asked wrapping his hands around my waist. He played back kissing me on the lips.

"Umm. I am not sure," I said with a chuckle.

"Well, when you make up your mind please let me know," he said slowly rubbing his tongue over my bottom lip.

"How will this work with me working for you and dating you?" I asked. My heart felt relieved to finally get what it wanted.

"You can still work for me but, I worry that you will grow tired of me and try to leave again," he said. He pushed my hair back away from my face.

"I think we should try to take it one day at a time and go from there," I said. I pulled his fingertips over to me as I walked over to the window.

"Why do you have such a big house if it's just you?" I asked.

"It is my inheritance from my parents," he said letting go of my fingers. He leaned against the wall and stared out the window. "I know this is all intimidating but, I want you here with me and right now I want you naked on the floor," he said planting another kiss on me. His tongue glided into my mouth massaging my tongue and lips. I gave into his request. I wrapped my hands around his waist and I pulled him closer to me. I could feel him ready for me. My body throbbed for him. I unzipped his pants and rubbed my hands over him. He closed his eyes and moaned. He lifted my shirt over my head throwing my shirt onto the floor. His hands cupped my breasts and my body ached intensively for him more. My breathing slowed as he kissed the back of my neck. His hand moved down my stomach causing me to flinch and giggle.

"You seem to be pretty ticklish around here," he said touching my stomach.

I bit my lip and tried not to laugh as he touched my belly. His slid his hands into my panties. I was happy that I was wearing an actually sexy pair. He fingers touched me and I almost exploded. I pushed his finger inside me and moaned.

"Gemma, you are very impatient today," he said pulling my panties down my legs. He placed his lips on my thighs sending me into quivers. I rubbed my fingers through his hair guiding his head gently back to where I was throbbing. I could barely stand without his help.

He made sure I was ready for him and tugged me onto the floor with him. I peeled his boxer briefs off him quickly. My body grew more impatient and I took lead. I straddled his manhood. My neck rolled as he placed his warm hands over my exposed breasts. He smiled as I moved up and down. He pulled me close to him kissing me and groaning into my mouth. My body erupted like a volcano and I let out a yelp.

He was calling out my name in just a matter of seconds. I collapsed onto his chest and kissed his neck as he still was inside me.

"So you think you want to move back in here when it is fixed?" he said playing with my hair.

"Hmm. No," I said.

He shifted his body releasing himself from me and we were lying face to face next to each other. "Why Gemma?" he asked. He acted like I told him he couldn't have a puppy.

"Well, I would rather be in your bed every night than in this big room all alone," I said biting the inside of my lip.

"I didn't think you wanted to be that close to me since you are still my assistant but, I would love that," he said.

"What should I tell my brother about us? He keeps warning me about you and that I should keep my head on straight and keep our relationship platonic," I said looking into his deep blue eyes.

He pushed himself onto his elbows from his back. He grabbed for his boxers and slacks. I really had a way with words. We were having a great time and I put my foot into my mouth.

"What did I say?" I asked pulling him back to me.

"Your brother Nate is right. If I were your brother I would tell you the same thing," he said careful not to look at me.

"Um, ok. Why should I not be involved with you?" I asked.

"Because we are not always what we seem to be," he said.

"What do you mean?" I asked.

"I did something really bad when I was in college and I don't want to talk about it right now," he said handing me my bra and underwear.

So this is it? I really had no secrets. I had told him about my sucky past and he was realizing my trust issues. I couldn't think of anything that would be that bad. Maybe Nate would tell me if he wouldn't. Is this the reason why he was so secretive with his friends?

I grew silent while I dressed. I sniffled swallowing my tears back.

"Gemma, please don't be upset. I am just not ready to talk about it yet," he said kissing my head.

"Is it that bad? So bad you can't tell me?" I choked out.

"I will tell you but, not today," he said.

I accepted his answer and we spent the evening his bedroom. I rested my head on his chest letting his heart beat be my clock. I closed my eyes and dreamt peacefully for once since I had begun working here.

Chapter 9

Back to work

I awoke to the sound of a mean Charlotte shooing me out of Will's bed. I rubbed the spot where Will was. It was just an empty cold spot on the bed.

"Ms. Carter it is time for work," she said pulling the blankets off me.

"What is the matter Charlotte?" I asked still holding the blanket by the hem.

"Gemma, I like you but I think you are stupid for getting involved with Master Campbell. He is a great employer but, you shouldn't be sleeping with him. I don't want to see you leave if things don't work out," she whispered.

"Charlotte don't be ridiculous. I can take care of myself," I said retrieving more of the blanket.

"Don't say I didn't warn you," she said leaving his room in a hurry.

What the hell was her problem? Why did everyone think I couldn't take care of myself? What bad secret was Will hiding from me that would change how I feel about him? I fell back onto the bed and let out a sigh.

A few minutes later Will came into his bedroom with breakfast and a toothy grin.

"Good morning beautiful, did you sleep well?" He asked gently pressing his lips to my forehead.

I pursed my lips together and gave a fake smile.

"You do know you have to get to work? Today," he said.

"Would it be ok if I took a shower first?" I asked. I dangled my feet over the edge of the bed and moved my breakfast tray to my other side.

"Eat first and shower. I will see you downstairs in my office later," he said kissing me.

"If you keep kissing me like that I will never report to work on time." I said.

He kissed me again and moved the food back toward me. I nibbled on a few pieces of bacon and picked a muffin. My head was spinning this morning as I tried to walk back to my pool house where my clothes were. I showered and dressed leaving my hair wet I rushed back to the main house to report to work.

Will was on a phone call and waved as I walked

provocatively by his office door. I smiled and opened the door to my office and sat at my desk. I was deep into emails when I felt Charlotte's eyes on me.

"Is everything ok?" I asked.

"Please think about what I said earlier. I apologize for being so rude about it. I guess I was just trying to be tough with you," she said in a hushed voice.

I nodded as confirmation that I would think about it. I was going to get to the bottom of this as soon as possible. The day went by answering calls, setting up private meetings, and canceling travel for Will.

He would be out next week for a few meetings. I could manage things while he was gone as long as Paul didn't surprise me. I had to keep Charlotte off my back and get information from Nate. I worked in some time for Nate and I to hook up for dinner next week and I planned on staying in the pool house until Will returned.

Will wined and dined me for the remainder of the week. He was going out of his way to make me feel like I was his girlfriend. He brought me flowers from his rose garden and even tried to buy me a new car. I wouldn't let him. I loved my trusty Jetta. I received an email from the decorator asking about the room and when to start. I forwarded it to Will since I had no idea where I was really going to stay. He called my name from the down the hall.

"Yes?" I said sitting on the leather chairs in front of him.

He got up and closed the door behind him latching the lock. He pulled me to standing and wrapped his hands around me. "You know I am completely smitten with you right?" he said kissing my lips on and off.

"I sure hope so," I said smiling.

"Come with me this week? Come with me to New

York," he said.

"Will, I made arrangements to see Nate and I still have to work and I don't want to feel like," I stumbled.

"Like what?" he asked pursing his lips together.

"Like I am sleeping with my boss," I blurted out.

"Well, you are sleeping with your boss and I don't care what other people say," Will said guiding me back to his desk. He moved papers off his desk and picked me up. I wrapped my legs around his waist. He placed my bum on his desk where he usually types away and answers phone calls yelling at some chump. He touched a button on his phone that went straight to voice mail. I moved a loose pen that was stuck under me. I was happy to be wearing a skirt today. It was easy access for Will. He moved his hand up my leg kissing it softly. He removed my shoes, which I was afraid my tired feet might smell after being stuck in a confined area for hours. Each kiss sent radiating chills over my skin. My nipples hardened which were noticeable through my tight blouse. Will pushed my skirt up more, tearing away my panties and discarding them to the floor. My breathing picked up and I allowed him total control over my body at that moment. He kissed up my legs teasing me. My body arched and I needed him now but he wanted to kill me slowly. He unbuttoned my blouse and kissed one breast and rubbed the other one with his large hand. As he planted warm kisses on me I ripped open his shirt. Buttons hit the floor and he looked at me raising his one brow. I rubbed my hands over his muscular chest and pulled him close to me. He had already managed to unhinge my bra releasing my heavy breasts. He threw it by my saturated panties. Here I was on his desk with nothing but a hiked up skirt. I kissed his mouth hard moaning into his mouth.

He was excited and dropped his pants and

boxers to the floor. I moved to the edge of desk. I pulled him close to me.

"You look so good Gemma," he said moving his hands all over my skin.

I blushed and kissed him more. I wrapped my legs around his waist pulling him towards me. He moved slowly into me. I let out a sigh as he moved in and out. I was on my elbows with my back arched. I have had sex with one guy besides Will and this was like everything that girls had talked about. He picked up his pace and I breathed faster. My body was building up again like a volcano and he must have sensed it and slowed down.

"We are not finished yet Gemma. Get down and turn around and place your hands on the desk," he said picking me up from his desk. My skirt was still around my waist. I did as I was told and spread my fingers out on his desk. He placed one of his hands over top mine. He kissed the back of my neck and slipped himself back inside me. I had never done it this way and my body was screaming for him at this point. My hands curled as he picked up his pace and I had to stand on my tiptoes. He grabbed my hair as he kissed me on the neck again. My blood raced through my veins and now his body was smacking behind me. I did everything I could not to be too vocal. He said my name into my ear as he climaxed and slowed down. I on the other hand was exhausted. I dropped from my tiptoes position and turned to face him. He grabbed some tissues and helped clean me up. I was still excited and his touch made me moan.

"Let me take care of you," he said placing me back on the desk. He gently moved my knees apart. I felt his warm breath on me and anticipation filled me. I grabbed his hair pulling him closer to me. He looked up to me with a wicked smile. His warm wet lips touched me and he moved his tongue in circular motions. It was not long and I was panting. He moved his fingers inside me still tonguing me. I slowed my breath until I erupted from pure ecstasy.

He moved back up to me and kissed me gently. I

could taste myself on him. I blushed as I realized what we had just done.

"Have I convinced you to come with me to New York?" he asked.

"Well, if you promise me that we will do that again. I might come a day late," I said. I retrieved my undergarments and blouse. I flattened out my skirt trying to rid it of wrinkles. I stepped into my heels as I pulled my hair behind my ears.

Will pulled his pants and boxers up in one step. I giggled as I watched him button up his tattered shirt.

"Here, let me help you," I said.

"You got my head all crazy and I can't even button my own shirt," he said rubbing my face with the outside of his hand.

"Maybe you should crack a window so, you can clear your head," I said jokingly.

We both had huge smiles as I helped him fix his desk back to the way it was before we done our business.

Chapter 10

Brotherly advice

Will had been gone for the week and I was supposed to meet up with him in New York tomorrow. I was missing him and feeling a bit lonely. I met up with Nate as he promised me he would. We met at a little sports bar downtown.

I sipped a beer as I waited for Nate. I dangled my legs under the table and stared at my phone in case Will decided to text me or call. Nate finally showed up late and flustered.

"Sorry, I am late just had to take care of some business," he said finishing a text on his cell phone.

"It's cool. I ordered some beers and nachos," I said.

"So what's been going on? Have you heard from mom or dad?" I asked.

"Um, no mom only calls when she is depressed and Dad is dad. He never calls," Nate said rolling his eyes.

"Same here except, she also calls me when she has been drinking her favorite wine," I said laughing.

"What is new with you?" Nate asked.

"Well, work is cool. Actually, I am going to New York tomorrow afternoon," I said.

The waitress brought us our beers and nachos. He of course flirted with the young girl thanking her for her good service. I almost gagged watching him.

"So, you are going to New York with Will?" he asked.

I took a sip of my beer. "He is already there working. I will be there to work tomorrow," I said tilting my head emphasizing the word work.

"You guys are sleeping together I guess," he said shoving a nacho into his mouth.

I almost spit out food across the table. "What?" I said

"Will sleeps with lots of women. I tried to warn you about him. He has a history of breaking hearts in college and I guess he didn't care you were my sister," he said wiping his mouth of cheese.

Um…. Was the only thing I could say. I shifted in the booth as I discussed my sex life with my brother.

"What do you mean he has a history with women?

Is there something I should know?" I asked. I knew damn well Nate knew more and was hesitating to tell me. Whatever they were hiding from me was certainly juicy.

"In college that is what you do. You find girls to be with but Will was totally gifted. He had sex with a professor once. One girl named Gina stalked him sophomore year," he said laughing.

"Well, Will is an adult now you don't think he is like that anymore do you?" I asked. My nachos were about to come back up. I was in a relationship with a sex addict. He knew all the right moves I guess from the tons of practice. I felt dirty and lost my appetite. I did however order another round of beers.

"You tell me. You so call work for him right?" he said using his fingers to quote the word work.

"I have only seen him with one other lady and," I hesitated mentioning myself.

"So, is he some sex addict or something," I

asked.

"All guys are sex addicts Gemma," Nate said laughing.

I agreed and sipped more of my beer and crossed my arms. "There is more you are not telling me isn't there?" I asked. Will loving sex wasn't enough to scare me away. I knew there had to be more.

"I can't be the one to tell you. Will has to tell you," he said pushing the plate of empty nachos to the middle of table.

"Is it that bad?" I asked.

"Look, you're my little sister and I don't want to see you hurt or ruin your life ok," he said.

I paid for dinner since Nate had helped me out when I was down and out. He hugged me and wished me luck. He also mentioned that if things get crazy to give him a call.

Chapter 11

Heights

I had only been on an airplane once and I was a child. My mind raced with all the bad things that could happen before we even took off. I gripped the arm of the seats as the plane ascended. I closed my eyes and breathed in through my nose and out from my mouth. Luckily, Will upgraded me to first class and when the plane had reached a steady form the stewardess offered me a drink. I happily obliged. Three drinks later I was relaxed and my head felt fuzzy. I ordered water the closer we came to New York.

Heading to baggage claim I saw a sign with Gemma Carter on it. The funny thing was it was Will dressed like his driver James. I laughed and caught up with him. He grabbed me and kissed me. It was a long slow kiss. Had he missed me in just the one day I was away from him. He took my bags for me and opened the back door for me.

"You want me to sit in the back?" I asked.

"Yes Ms. Carter," he said with a smile.

He shut the door after I made myself comfortable in the back seat. I was distracted by how good he looked. The bright lights of New York were not even important to me. I stared at him in the rear view mirror. I caught him a few times glancing at me in it. I wanted him right now. I kept my eyes on him the whole way to the hotel. He parked the car and opened the door for me.

"Ms. Carter, you will be staying in my room

tonight if that is okay with you," he said.

I removed his silly driver hat and placed it on my own head and we walked hand and hand into the hotel. The front desk gave a nod to Will and he smiled. The elevator was packed with people standing way to close to each other. We managed to squeeze in until we reached the floor his room was on.

He pulled me by the hand to the room of his door. The door hadn't even closed and we were kissing passionately dropping my bags on the floor.

"Hey, watch it I have perfume in there," I said chuckling.

"I'll buy you more," he said moving his lips down my neck.

I could tell the room was enormous out the slits of my eyes. The large windows caught my eyes and were instantly pulled over to it. They overlooked the heart of the city. It was breathtaking but he quickly pulled me back to him.

My eyes argued with my body. My body won and I followed him to the bedroom. He took off the ridiculous driver outfit and he let me unbutton his shirt and take his slacks off. It took him only seconds to undress me. The cool air sent chills over my skin and he rubbed his fingertips over me lightly. He lay over top of me kissing me and running his tongue up and down my body. We made love that night and when his body spasmed, he whispered my name it into my ear. My body lay exhausted and famished but my mind was so delighted.

He immediately cleaned up and showered as I took a catnap in the buff. The only thing covering me was a sheet. He came out of the bathroom in only a towel. Water ran down his muscular physique. He smelled of soap and cologne and it reminded me that I also needed to bathe. The warm water made me more aware that I was starving and to take it easy on the alcohol until I got more food in me.

"Let's go," Will yelled outside the bathroom

door.

"Just a minute, Sheesh," I said drying off.

I walked out to retrieve my wardrobe and he was by the window sipping champagne. He was dressed in a tuxedo. He looked absolutely insatiable. I stood on my tiptoes to kiss him still dripping.

"We are going to be late if we keep doing this," he said grabbing my backside.

"Okay, Stop distracting me," I joked.

I slipped into a black cocktail dress with a hem that stopped just an inch or so above the knee. I made sure to wear high enough heels so I would be tall and close enough to Will's face. I swept my hair up in a French twist and embellished it with a silver flower hairpiece that locked in the twist. I wore my eye makeup heavy with dark cat eyes but kept my lips light with some red toned gloss. I sprayed perfume on my wrists and neck. I stared at the woman that I saw reflected back at me she was unrecognizable. I was not the same pathetic girl who was heartbroken. I was successful and worked for a hot guy who I happened to be sleeping with. I would have never imagined a life like this especially someone like me.

I opened the door from the bathroom and saw Will on his phone. His back was turned and he was talking quietly. He was hissing and was agitated from the caller. I tip toed careful not to disturb him. I grabbed my earrings and necklace. He must have seen me and said bye to the caller and shoved the phone in his pocket.

"Everything ok Will?" I asked trying to clasp my necklace behind my neck.

"Here let me help you," he said brushing his fingers over my neck. His touch electrified through my spine. He ignored my last question and got my necklace on. He kissed my neck and turned me around. Just a simple kiss on the back of my neck sent volts of electricity through me.

"You look beautiful Gemma. I better be careful

and keep you close to me tonight," he said with a wink.

Chapter 12

Old friends

Thirty minutes later we were in his private car with dark windows. The driver opened the door for me and Will was on the sidewalk holding his hand out for me. We entered a big glass encased building. The floors were covered in dark marble. Two men stood on each side of double doors that opened up to a ballroom. Antique chandeliers hung from the ceiling and were dimly lit. It was like a scene from a fairy tale. People were seasoned throughout the huge room. Will kept me on his arm close to him like he said. We walked through the dining area near the bar until he noticed a friend. He introduced me to some older gentlemen that began flirting with me.

"It was good seeing John," Will said shaking his hand. He moved on to other crowds of people. I tried hard to keep a fake smile as he introduced me to people who I have spoken to over the phone and through emails. My feet began to ache and I was ready to sit.

"Would you like something to drink?" Will asked.

"Yes, I would love one," I said. I felt kind of weird mixing my business with my love life. I felt dirty and all these people knew it now or was I just being paranoid? Will held me by the fingertips as he led me to the bar. I watched the dance floor as people slowed danced to classical music.

"Gemma Carter is that you?" an unfamiliar voice asked.

I raised my brow and turned toward the man. I studied his face to see who he was. He was about my age in his twenties but not in his late twenties like Will. He put his hand out and I returned to shake it but he kissed my hand. I blushed still not recognizing him.

"Gemma, it's me Jeremy Wilkins from high school," he said. *Oh my god?* He was a friend with the one guy I dated in high school.

"Hey Jeremy, it's great to see you. What are you doing here?" I asked him. Where was Will with those drinks? I looked nervously over to Will at the bar and he was talking to some woman. Her dress had no back on it and he had his hand on her.

"Well, my company helped put this event together," he said with a smile. According to my memory Jeremy was now taller and better looking. He was a bit shorter in high school covered with acne and wore band shirts all the time. He was a close friend to the guy I lost my virginity to and he probably got to hear all about the crappy experience.

"Your company?" I asked in amazement.

"Yeah, after high school I went to college and met some people who had the same idea as me about Public Relations and we started a business," he said.

"Well, it looks awesome," I said moving my eyes back to Will.

"So, what are you doing here? I saw you with William Campbell. Are you two an item?" he asked.

I was just as confused as he was about my status since Will was getting friendly with some lady at the bar. "Well, I work for him and let me attend as his so called date tonight," I said trying to be funny. I rolled my neck, as I felt uncomfortable talking about my love life to an old high school friend.

"He is one lucky guy," he said staring at me.

I blushed and looked around nervously. Thanks Jeremy, Have a good night," I said holding my hand to shake his. Jeremy grabbed my hand and kissed it again. He slid past my side whispering to me, "You look beautiful."

I smiled and headed to the bar. Will hadn't even noticed me beside him at the bar. I gave him the same treatment. Will's back still turned from me I signaled for the bartender. I looked over to Will and he was very close to the leggy blonde with the revealing dress. She was almost sitting on his lap and her breasts were practically out of her dress. My feet screamed to get out of my heels so I sat at the other side of the bar to relieve them. I rolled my ankles and took a long swig of my drink. A drink later and with Will forgetting me I was ready to go. I wasn't going to be all-desperate and ask for Will's attention. I wasn't mad, as a matter of fact, I was infuriated. I threw my rule out about drinking before eating. My drinks gave me some fake confidence and I walked away from the bar to watch people dance. It was like a scene out of a movie. Men dressed in tuxedos dancing with beautiful women dressed in their best gowns. As I watched them move, I knew I was nothing like any of them. A familiar voice broke me from stressed thoughts. Things were definitely not looking up at this point.

"Gemma, Would you like to dance?"

Paul stood beside me in a tuxedo like the other men. *How does this man find me everywhere I go? He must have a tracking device planted on me.* I looked back at Will who was still busy with blondie at the bar. "Umm. Surc," I said hesitating.

He touched the small of my back and held my hand with his. "You know if you were mine I wouldn't be talking to some other woman," he said looking over at Will.

I smiled and said, "Well, I am not yours so,

no need to worry."

"You know it won't last long?" he said moving to other side of the dance floor.

"What won't last long?" I asked.

"You and Will of course and you resisting me?" he said twirling me. "I mean look at you. This is the second time you have danced with me. How many times have you danced with Will?" he asked. "What will it take to get you to be with me?" he asked.

I had to give it to Paul he was confident but, he was arrogant. "Paul, it will be a cold day in hell when I sleep with you," I said.

The song ended and I let go of him and stood by the edge of the dance floor. He followed me and whispered in my ear. "A man can dream can't he?" he said and left the floor.

I laughed and searched for my boss again. I walked back to the bar and he and the sexy blonde were gone. "Great," I mumbled under my breath. I'm stuck here in a room full of clients and colleagues looking desperate and lonely.

Was Will just using me until something better came along? He said he loved me but was that just in the heat of the moment? I had another drink and I needed to freshen up. I found the restrooms near the bar and I found something else too. I found two well-dressed adults making out by the bathrooms in the dark. I didn't have to look to know it was Will and blondie. My drinks rose in the back of my throat. I ran into the bathroom and threw up. Tears fell from my eyes. How could I have been so stupid? I should have listened to all the warnings from my brother. I flushed the toilet and fixed my face up. I took a few deep breaths and got out my phone and called the hotel and set up for another room. I made sure it came from Will's pocket since he was dicking me over. I now had a separate room and later I would fix my flight home. I shoved my phone in my clutch purse and retrieved my gloss. I left the ladies room and Will and blondie had ventured off somewhere else. I headed to the double doors where I had entered and had the valet hail me a cab.

Chapter 13

Planes and enemies

I got into the cab and shut the door. Will yelled for me but, I now had the upper hand and I was playing the same game as him. I was at the hotel in a matter of minutes. I called the airline and rearranged my flight home. I got one leaving in a few hours. It was hard to get and terribly expensive but, I didn't care because he was paying for it. Just like I was paying for being his assistant.

Before, Will had gotten back to the hotel I managed to get my things from his room. I was packed and down in the lobby. Will was down stairs talking to the receptionist. He hadn't noticed me and I tried to slide past him but the front desk wished me a good day. Damn it. I was so close to going unnoticed.

"Ms. Carter, there you are," He said grabbing me by the elbow.

"What the hell are you doing?" he asked.

"I am going home. I have to get back to work. My boss doesn't like when I am late," I said trying to shake his grip from me.

"Well, your boss doesn't like the game you are playing," he said.

"I know a few things my boss does like," I said sarcastically.

"Is that so," he asked pulling me outside.

"I know you love blonde bimbos," I said. He

said nothing in return because he knew I saw him.

He adjusted stance and hailed a cab.

"What are you doing? Where is your stuff?" I asked.

"They are sending it to the airport," He said pushing me into the cab. I pushed his hands off me.

"I saw you two tonight," I said. "Next time could you not embarrass me by asking me to an event as your date while you fuck another woman there," I said.

The cab driver looked at me in the mirror. I didn't care I was pissed and I hated being in the car with Will.

"Is this what it is going to be like? I am only good enough for you at home where nobody has to actually see me," I asked.

"Gemma, I don't know what to say," he said rubbing the back of his neck.

"You don't have to say anything. I should have

known better than to sleep with you since you are my boss," I said raising my voice. The driver raised his eyebrows enjoying our crazy show.

"Gemma, stop making a scene." Will said shushing me.

"Are you serious? You are worried about me making a scene?" I said sarcastically. "You had sex in a hallway at a charity event. You are something you know that? When we get to the airport you don't know me and I will be moving out and giving you my letter," I said pointing at him.

"Gemma. Please calm down. Can we talk about this when we don't have an audience?" he said looking at the cab driver.

"No," I said firmly.

I grabbed my bags and headed for the terminal and I made sure that I took a different plane than him but that son of a bitch was good. He weaseled his way onto my flight and the seat next to me.

I tried my hardest to ignore him. I wanted to cry but I didn't want him to see me. I closed my eyes as the plane tilted into the air for takeoff. My heart raced and my palms began to sweat. As I had my panic attack Will took my hand. I shoved him off me.

"Don't touch me," I hissed.

"Stop it Gemma, for gods sake act like an adult," he said.

I was fuming. I peered through my lashes "Excuse me," I said.

"Act like an adult? Who the hell do you think you are? Oh, I can fuck whoever and pretend I am in love with my friend's sister who happens to be my assistant," I said mockingly.

"I am saying you are screaming at me like a child that didn't get her way," he said shifting towards me.

The stewardess gave Will a way too friendly

smile and offered him a beverage not even noticing my existence. I talked over top of her; "We will have two scotch on the rocks I ordered." And I turned to him and said, "What will you be having the stewardess in that tiny ass bathroom?"

Will creased his brow and looked to the flight attendant "Excuse her she hit her head earlier. Would you mind bringing us some mimosas and waters?" he said. He plastered a fake smile that charmed the flight attendant away.

"Gemma, you are going to get us kicked off the flight if you don't behave," he said through his teeth.

"Just so you know, when we are back home I am leaving. I am looking for another job and place to live," I said looking out the window.

"I understand you are upset with me but, that doesn't mean you should quit. I really need your help," he said grabbing my hand.

"Don't touch me Will or should we go back to

being formal?" I said.

"Look, what happened last night is complicated," he said pinching the bridge of nose.

"Hmm. I really don't think it could be that complicated. Oh do I sleep with some blonde and fuck up my current relationship or do I stay with my date and be monogamous," I said rolling my eyes. "Seriously, how stupid do you think I am? You know what, don't answer that. I should have listened to the warnings from everyone," I said shifting myself away from him.

"Look, if I told you, I don't think you would understand. I am sure all the warnings are probably for good reason and you should have listened to them," he said.

"So, that is it? You are just going keep me in the dark about everything? Besides the obvious why is everyone warning me about you and what's with blondie last night?" I asked.

The flight attendant came and interrupted our

conversation once more. She gave me the evil eye as she passed me my drinks. I thanked her for her service praying she would go away from us.

Will downed his mimosa as I sipped on mine. I hated orange juice but, this had alcohol in it and I needed something to chill me out.

"I will tell you if you can act like an adult about it," He said.

I rolled my eyes and waved for him to continue.

"Blondie is Maggie. We met during college. She has a reputation of being easy to take to bed but I like a challenge. After a few years of trying to get with me she got dirt on me and started black mailing me. In return for her not to make my private personal life public I pay her with sex," he said.

I let out a little chuckle. "Are you being serious?" I asked.

"Very serious?" he said.

"What is so bad you don't want public to everyone?" I asked.

He sighed and said, "Everything people are warning you about."

"That is all you are going to say? No explanation, not even a hint?" I asked. He definitely let curiosity take the best of me. I knew this flight would be a little longer and maybe with a couple more drinks he would confess his dirt to me.

I had apologized to the flight attendant and slipped her a fifty-dollar bill. Her service was immaculate. Will stayed tight-mouth most of the flight after he spoke about Maggie. Something was off still about him though.

"Just tell me so we can clear the air," I said.

"I am afraid to tell you?" he said.

He kept his voice low and didn't look at me.

"Why? I can't go running anywhere," I said with a little smile.

"You will leave once this flight lands and I don't know if I can deal with that," he said. His jaw clenched and he rubbed his hands together.

We sat in silence for a couple of minutes. I was contemplating my next move after we got back. I was sure I was going to end our sensual relationship but I could still work for him.

The captain speaking interrupted our silence. He just let us know that we would be arriving in an hour.

"She found out I slept with a professor for money to start up my business," he said in a whisper. "Trust me it's not something I am proud of and I didn't want the professor to lose her job," he said.

Wow. He really does have some type of

reputation. Is that why he is now a hermit working from home? Most guys wouldn't care about scoring with a teacher but what was so different? "Well, why does it matter now? You are an adult and have been out of college for years now," I said.

"I made a big mistake Gemma. I got her pregnant," he said.

My mouth dropped opened. *Oh my god.* "So, you have a kid?" I asked.

"Umm. No she ugh got an abortion," he said. His face went pale as he spoke of his past.

"Well, why does Maggie know about this?" I asked.

"Maggie caught me kissing the teacher and threatened to give us away," he said.

"So, why now? Why are you letting her in your pants for something that happened years ago?" I asked. I didn't understand his hang up from the past. Why was he letting Maggie have control over him? He was always in control when it came to the ladies.

"She has since then been trying to work for me and I refuse to work with her. She is relentless. She wants to break my world. When she saw you last night she attacked me at the bar. She said she was going to out my reputation once more for sleeping with my employees," he said.

"I don't give a shit what she says. You still didn't have to sleep with her. I thought we had something together. I guess maybe I was a fool for being your personal assistant but I need the job. I am not sure if I can do this anymore Will. You are making me a feel like a train wreck. My emotions are crazy and we have only just started," I said fighting back my tears.

"I meant what I said the other night Gemma," he said. "I love you but I come with baggage,"

That was all he was going to give me. You can either take it or leave it act. "Will, I am afraid if I get any closer you are going to hurt me with your womanizing," I said.

"Womanizing? I am only with you and as far as Maggie goes, I already explained it to you," he said leaning in closer to my face.

"If this is true then I want you to end your relationship with Maggie. We will figure this all out together. We can hire a lawyer to protect your business and your life," I said grabbing his hand.

"I wish it was that simple. I can't ruin anybody else's life," he said.

"We can figure it out but, you can't be with Maggie anymore if you are going to be with me," I said. I was laying down the ultimatum but I haven't felt that way about a man as I did with Will. I loved him. I loved being with him. I loved his touch and how when not distracted by Maggie, made me feel important.

"Let me think this over and get in touch with

some people ok?" he said.

We didn't talk the remainder of the flight. We did hold hands. I still wanted to keep our relationship on hold until he figured things out. My head felt fuzzy from mimosas and the thought of Will being a father.

I really didn't know much about Will other than my own personal observations. He could be very generous and he was good to his help. I didn't know much about his family history.

The plane landed and we retrieved our bags. James was waiting for us in the terminal and so was Julie.

Chapter 14

Julie

The airport was crowded and I could barely walk through without saying excuse me a hundred times. My chest pounded and I curled my fist up when I saw her. She saw me with Will and I felt like I gave her a big middle finger. What was she doing standing next to James? I prayed that she would walk away but she didn't. She did the exact opposite.

"Long time no see," I said to the Bitch

disguised as a woman. It took all the energy I had to contain myself in the airport.

"I happened to be here when I saw you. Then I saw your friend here and umm," She said putting out her hand to shake with Will.

"Will this is Julie my former roommate," I said raising my brow. He must have sensed me being uncomfortable. She had a lot of audacity approaching me after what she had done. Just like her she acted like it had never happened. She was ready to put her claws into Will. I was in no mood to play nice and I had been drinking. James took my bags relieving my tired hands.

"It is nice to meet you Julie but, Gemma and I are in a bit of a hurry," he said shaking her hand. He was polite but firm.

She shot me a look. She didn't like being second best to anyone especially to me. She took everything I had and fucked it literally. I prayed in my head that she would take her pathetic self and walk away.

"I don't mean to hold you up but I saw you and wanted to say hello. I am glad I got to meet you Mr." she said.

"It's Mr. Campbell and I apologize but, I do have to go, like I said we are in a hurry," he said walking towards the doors that lead outside. I gave her a wicked smile and started to follow him. Julie grabbed my arm and whispered under her breath.

"Be careful not to lose him to some other lady Gemma. He is quite a catch. Women will be lining up to be with that one. It is definitely an upgrade from Ben," she said raising her brow.

I pulled my arm away from her and gave her my keep your hands off me look. I stormed off to find Will waiting for me in the car. James held the door open for me and shut it behind me.

I looked back at the doors and Julie stood there waving at me. My face warmed and I gritted my teeth.

"So that was the infamous Julie," he said with a chuckle.

"It's not funny and yes it was. She is ready to jump you by the way," I said. He laughed back at me. He grabbed my hand and pushed a button to give us privacy from James.

"Julie is confident I will give her that. She isn't quite my type. I don't have sex with every woman that wants to have sex with me. I like a challenge. I like you and I want you to forget about the last few days and Julie. I want you to keep working for me and live back in the main house," he said rubbing his finger over my whitened knuckles.

"You are giving me a roller coaster head trip. You have to make a few adjustments if you want me back in your bed," I said.

"State your requests Ms. Carter," he said

turning to me.

"No more Maggie or any other women. Stay away from Julie and anything she offers you. Also, when you invite a woman to an event where she is dressed up, you should keep your creepy horny friends away from her," I said.

"I assume you are talking about Paul?" he asked. His face changed when he said Paul's name.

"What is it with Paul anyways? Why is he always trying to get in my panties?" I asked.

Will moved his hands onto my thighs and leaned in close to my face. I could smell the orange juice from the mimosas. "Paul wants everything I have. He can be very competitive and will try very hard to get you. That is why I will say this one more time. Stay away from him. He has a reputation as a cruel man to women," he said nipping my lips with his teeth.

"I know someone like that," I said kissing him

back.

"You do? Who?" he asked moving his hands in between my legs. I panted as he began rubbing his hands on me.

"Stop Will," I said.

"Why? I want you right here in my car," he said as he slid his hand under my shirt. My body was screaming for him.

"I know but, I am still mad," I said trying to catch my breath.

His mouth moved onto my neck and I began to lie back on the seat. "I agree to your terms," he said kissing my breasts. He hit another button and told James to drive until he called him again.

His fingers moved down into my pants. I was ready for him and I moaned as he slid his fingers in and out of me. I began to pull his pants down rubbing his manhood through his boxer briefs. He pulled my panties down and began kissing me. I bit my hand to keep quiet knowing James could probably hear us.

I pulled the remainder of his clothes off. He was on top of me thrusting me. I whimpered with joy. How could I stay mad at this beautiful man? He was a package though and so was I. He collapsed onto me after he climaxed and kissed me. I slowly got my clothes and began to dress.

"Don't dress yet," he said staring at me.

"Why? I am sure James is tired of driving around the city," I said with a smile.

"That is what he gets paid to do Gemma. I want to look at you naked in the back of my car. I want you to sit here," he said patting the black leather seat.

I placed my clothes back on the floor and did as commanded. He was still excited and ready for more. I wrapped my arms around myself trying to keep warm.

"Cold?" he asked.

I nodded and he began to kiss me again. He got on the floor of the car by my feet. He slowly kissed up my calf and I pulled back realizing I needed to shave. Gently he pulled my leg back to him. I squeaked a bit when he kissed the back of it. My body started to melt as his warm mouth moved up my thighs. He pulled me to the edge of the seat and commanded me to lay back. He spread my legs apart and kissed me. He moved his tongue in circular motions until my body tensed and I let out a moan. God Will was good at that. I had never climaxed until I met him.

Chapter 15

Trouble

Things were getting back to normal for me. Will and I had plenty of make up sex and I was busy back at work. I stayed up late working for Will setting up last minute things for a new company he was thinking about starting. I worked on my computer until my eyes hurt. The phone rang and broke me out my trance. The number flashed on my phone as unrecognized. I hesitated to answer it but I did. I should have went with my gut and not answered it because it was Paul. How did he get my number? What the hell did he want? I made a few guesses of my own of course.

"Hello Gemma. How are you?" he asked.

"Who is this?" I asked.

"Your dance partner and your shoulder to cry on," he said. Was he being serious? I couldn't believe this guy.

"Don't you have some other woman to pester or shall I say stalk?" I said sarcastically.

"You think I stalk you?" he asked.

"Ugh Yeah," I said.

"Well, I just wanted to see how things were since your boss slash lover was fucking another woman," he said. His words cut me. He played a dirty game and I despised him for that. "If you are ever looking for another job I have opening,"

"Great I will keep that in mind. Is that all Paul?" I said through my teeth. This guy never gives up. He just hit me below the belt with the Maggie thing and now my head was hurting.

"Yeah, one more thing, if things don't work out between you and Will, promise me you will come see me," he said in a low voice.

"Bye Paul," I said hanging up on him.

My head pounded more and felt like I was going to be sick. Will came into my office to bring me to bed. He carried me to his room and lied me on the bed. It was the first night we didn't make love. Which was probably a good idea since Paul had just called me and it made me feel sicker.

I fell asleep in Will's arms. I felt so safe but I could feel things changing. I was blind to the fact he had a reputation of being with lots of women. Days went by and he pulled further away from me. My headaches increased more and I felt like sleeping more.

Will walked by my office not even looking at me. I pinched the bridge of my nose and let out a sigh. I followed Will to his office shutting the doors behind me.

"Alright, what is going on? You done with me so I get the cold shoulder?" I asked.

"No baby. I just have a lot going on and you have been not feeling well," he said flopping into his chair.

"What is it then? Out with it," I demanded.

"Maggie is trying to go public about my affair with my professor alright," he snapped.

"You couldn't just tell me that? You have been ignoring me and barely looking at me," I said. I could feel the water in my eyes collect. Was he rejecting me again? I couldn't do this anymore. I couldn't be what he wanted me to.

"She is making things complicated and I am having a hard time with all this," he said.

Will's body was stiffened and he grew agitated with me. I came over to him and lay my hands on his shoulders. I rubbed his neck to relax him and he placed his hand over top of mine, the first real acknowledgement in days from him.

"Maybe I can help you relax," I suggested. I rubbed my hands down his chest over his muscles. He turned his chair around to me. He tried to stand but I pushed him back down. I wanted to take the lead this time. I wanted him to do what I say.

I unbuttoned his pants rubbing him until his eyes rolled back. I moved his underwear down to his ankles. I kissed his stomach teasing him with my tongue. He was ready for me and guided my head down to him. I gave him long wet kisses over his erection. He moaned louder grabbing my hair. I pushed him deep in mouth and moved my tongue around. I used my other hand to keep him wet and slick. He stiffened and let out a gasp.

"Oh my god Gemma I love you," he said.

The words I heard after sex was the reminder that I had made my man happy. He was zipping up his pants when there was a knock at the door. Charlotte's low voice talked through the door. "Ms. Carter there is a Julie Bowers here to see you,"

My head began to pound again like a jackhammer.

I flattened out my shirt and pants. I wiped my mouth off knowing I smelled like Will. I hissed for Will to get dressed and I walked out down the hall to the front door. Julie stood in her nice tight dress that accentuated her curves. Was she trying to make me jealous of her?

"May I help you Julie?" I asked.

"I wanted to apologize for the other day and for the whole Ben thing," she said.

"You could have emailed this to me or wrote a letter." I said. I knew exactly why she was here. She was hoping to see Will again. I just wished I knew how the hell she found out where he lived. His company's headquarters is downtown where he should be working.

"Well, I wanted to be a little personal since the whole Ben thing and then I was kind of nasty at the airport. To be quite honest with you I am a bit jealous of you Gemma," She said looking down at the ground.

It may be the words I longed to hear from Julie but, they were not sincere and I wasn't buying it. "Ok, then let's try to move on in our lives," I said trying to hurry the conversation.

"Gemma," a deep voice yelled.

"Just a minute sir," I yelled back.

"Sir, what do you work for him Gemma?" Julie asked with a big crooked smile. What was she planning? She was ready to sink her nails into him and I was not going to let that happen. She screwed up enough things in my life. She was the wicked witch and I was Dorothy. Man, do I wish I had a pair of ruby slippers right about now.

"That is none of your business Julie and I have to go," I said slowly pushing the door shut.

"Gemma, you are one lucky bitch. I meant what I said I am sorry. I really don't know how you stayed with Ben so long he became quite boring," she said holding her handbag.

"Is there a problem Gemma," said Will. He was wearing his crisp white button down shirt and dark slacks.

"No sir, Julie was just leaving," I said holding my hand out to shake.

She shook my hand keeping her eyes on Will. "It was great to see you Gemma and it was a pleasure to see you again too," she said pursing her lips together.

"Have a nice day," I said and shut the door. I leaned my back against the door and let out a sigh.

"What the hell was that?" Will asked.

"Apparently an apology but it was her way to

see you. She wants to size you up so she can sleep with you. That is what she is good at," I said rolling my eyes.

"I don't think that will happen. She is kind of appalling if you ask me," he said.

"Well, she likes what I have and will stop at nothing to get her way," I said.

Will wrapped his arms around my waist and kissed my forehead. "I don't want her. I only want you," he said with a little smile.

I still tasted him. His scent intoxicated me and I stood on my tiptoes and kissed him. This kiss was different it was a controlling kiss. I wanted to show him that he belonged to me. I left him standing in the hall as I walked back to my office. I wanted him to long for me the rest of the day. I wanted him to be distracted and be ready for me.

The day went on and Will kept walking by my office. He acted like he was doing something with the printer. I laughed to myself as he played his little game. I tried to not let Julie put a damper on my day but she had definitely distracted me. What was she up to? How did she find where I worked?

He walked by my office again and he stopped and pulled the doors shut behind him. "Ms. Carter you can go early today," he said with a smile.

"Thank you Mr. Campbell. Is everything ok? I mean you usually don't let me go home early," I said with a chuckle. I shut my laptop and turned towards Will.

"I am having a hard time concentrating after our meeting this morning and then you left me hanging in the hallway with that kiss," He said. Will moved over to me and sat on my desk. He crossed his feet and arms. He had the biggest grin plastered on his face.

"What?" I asked.

"You," he said.

My face warmed as he stared at me. "You are making me blush Will," I said.

"I know. Gemma, go upstairs and get naked in my bed with me," he demanded.

"You are such the romantic," I said laughing. I got up from my desk and kissed him like I did in the hallway earlier. I pulled him by the collar to follow me.

I opened the door to see Charlotte in the hallway. She was holding a basket of laundry and when she saw me she dropped it. "Here let me help you Charlotte," I said.

"No ma'am that is my job," she said shoving the clothes into the basket and rushing down the hall.

I looked at Will through the corner of my eye. *What was her problem? Had she been listening?* Will grabbed me by the waist and threw me over his shoulder. He was carrying me to the bedroom. This was the best job ever.

Charlotte's behavior changed more so over the next few weeks. She ignored me at all costs. I must have embarrassed her the other day. I wanted to make it up to her so I asked Will to give her the day off with pay since she had been working so hard. The strangest thing was she seemed mad about it. She grew more distant from me since then.

I gave her the space she needed and tried not to interfere anymore. She even became cold to Charles the butler. He didn't say much to me about it but did mention it to Will. Will didn't pay much attention to it since she still did her job well.

Chapter 16

Christmas

Christmas was coming and I wanted to get a present for Will. What do you get the man that has everything? I planned some time with him in a resort in Cabo San Lucas. I bought the tickets and wrapped them in a box. I slipped the box on his desk while he was grabbing a cup of coffee. I watched him walk past my office. I smiled and waved at him.

He stopped and backed up looking at me. “What?” he asked.

I just shrugged my shoulders. “Nothing,” I said and I began to type away.

He walked back to his office and shut the door. The minutes felt like forever as I waited for his reaction. My telephone rang and Will’s voice ordered me to his office. I hung up and sprinted to his office.

“You know you don’t have to call me on the phone. I am literally in the next room,” I said laughing.

“Gemma, What is this?” he asked inspecting the box.

“It is just a little present for my boss slash boyfriend,” I said rocking on my toes. “Hope you like it,"

"Well, I wasn't going to give you your gift until Christmas morning but, what the hell," he said pulling something out of his desk.

It was a rectangular shaped box wrapped with a red satin bow. I carefully untied the bow and opened the spring box. Staring back at me was a diamond necklace. I never owned any jewels that were real. It was beautiful. I took it out carefully holding it. I moved my hair to the side of my neck so Will could help put it on. He latched the necklace kissing my neck sending electricity throughout out my body.

"Your turn, open your present," I said anxiously.

He pulled the ribbon bow and opened the box. He pulled the envelope out that had our itinerary in it. "Gemma, this is awesome," he said reading it.

"I get you all to myself for a whole week without work related stuff," he said as he came over to me and kissed me.

"I made sure there were no meetings and I even let the staff off for that week. I hope that is ok with you," I said.

"If you are happy I am happy," he said.

We finished out our workweek. Friends stopped by to see Will and to give gifts. One night as he worked late I answered a low knock at the door. I opened the door and regretted it. Paul stood there with gifts in his hands and a Santa hat.

"Merry Christmas Gemma. Where is your boss?" he

asked giving me his creepy smile.

"He is in his office. Let me go get him," I said.

He pulled me by the elbow and placed his mouth on mine. He slid his tongue over mine and for one moment I didn't resist. Oh my god. I pushed him away and stormed to get Will. I knocked hard on Will's office door and looked to the other side of the hall. Charlotte was standing there again. When our eyes met she took off. She saw what happened. I couldn't believe Paul. Will came out of his office smiling and I pointed towards the door.

"Your friend Paul is here to see you," I said and walked to the bathroom.

I locked the door behind me and ran the water in the sink. I tried to catch my breath and not cry. I couldn't believe he kissed me. I contemplated telling Will. What would he do? Would he believe me? Paul has always been trying to get with me. Then there was Charlotte. She ran off when she knew I saw her watching me. I took deep breaths and came out of the bathroom.

"Gemma, won't you join us for a drink," Will said.

"Umm, I am not feeling that well. I think I may go lay down," I said rubbing my hands together.

"Should I send Charlotte up with some soup?" he asked.

"No, I will be ok," I said quickly.

I couldn't let him know that his friend had kissed me. I felt dirty and didn't want to be touched. I pushed Will away for the first time in months.

"Sorry, Will I am just not feeling all myself right now," I said turning away from him in the bed.

He let out a big sigh and turned to sleep. When I got up the next morning he was already working downstairs. I reported to my office and checked my emails. Nate sent Will and me an evite to meet at Mackey's for New Years. I got up from my desk and walked to Will's office. Charlotte stood there dusting the mantle and I smiled at her. She just looked back down at the mantle. "Okay," I mumbled under my breath.

I knocked before entering his office. My jaw dropped open as I saw Julie sitting in the leather chair. "Excuse me, I didn't know you had company," I said leaving the room.

I wanted to scream. My adrenaline pumped through my veins and my hands began to shake. What was she doing here? I closed the doors to my office and locked them. I sat on the floor rocking back and forth and began to cry. Was he mad at me because I didn't make love to him last night?

I heard her fake laugh in the hall and the muted conversation. It drove me mad. My fingernails dug into the palm of my hands. I wanted to go out there and deck her. I finally got up and wiped off my tears. I spent the remainder of my day locked in my office. Will knew I was upset but maybe that was his intention. I worked up my courage to leave the tiny office that was now feeling like it was closing in on me.

I walked to knock on Will's door. "Come in," he said before I made a sound.

"What the hell are you doing Will?" I demanded.

"Julie has been inquiring about a new position in my company and I wanted to see her credentials and interview her," he said looking at some papers on his desk.

"So this is it? I don't make love once and you kick me to the curb? Well, the hell with you and this job. Just so you know your creepy friend Paul kissed me last night and that is why I didn't have drinks and have sex with you," I said storming off.

"I heard quite the opposite story," Will hissed through his teeth.

"Fuck off Will," I said stomping up the steps.

I found the tickets I bought for us on his nightstand and tore them up. I grabbed my bags and packed them. I rolled my bag heavily down the steps almost falling as it rolled.

I threw my bag into my Jetta and left. I went to the only place I could. I went to my brother Nate's apartment.

"It was only a matter of time before this happened," Nate said.

"Why do you say that?" I asked.

He poured me a glass of wine and laughed to himself. "Will and Paul are both used to getting what they want. They are spoiled. We Carter's have had to work hard for everything. We appreciate things differently including our love life," he said.

He threw a blanket from his closet at me. I could sleep on the couch for a few days and see what happens. Will didn't call me and Paul wouldn't stop calling me. I thought about changing my number but it wouldn’t matter.

Chapter 17

The End is near

It had only been a few days and Nate reminded me that New Years was coming and I should try to get out of the house and have some fun. I thought it over and headed to the mall to find an outfit. I found a pair of tight black jeans, heels, and a trendy blouse. I didn't want to run into Will or Paul but, if I did I wanted to show them both what they were missing.

I drove Nate to the bar that night. Mackey's was crowded and I kept to myself at the bar. Music played loudly and people danced but it didn't faze me. The only thing that got me to move was when Will walked through the door with Julie. I started pounding beers then moved to shots. As I drank my misery away Mr. Creepy Paul approached me.

"Gemma, Happy New Years," he said.

I nodded and raised my shot glass. I spun around and watched Will with Julie.

"What is it about her," I asked.

Paul stood there staring at Julie. "Well, she has nice tits and she is pretty but, you are way hotter than her," he said. I had to give it to Paul. He knew if he wanted to attack he was going about it the right way tonight. He knew to wait for the girl to feel down and he would pick her up.

I watched Will across the room as he placed his hands over her legs. Nate must have seen me and told me he would take me home or call a cab if I was upset. I stayed. I wanted to see that asshole one last time. He looked at me and then kissed her in front of me. I spun in my bar seat and called for another shot. My vision began to blur and I was ready to go home.

"Gemma, you need a ride home?" Paul asked.

"I brought my car but, you can drive it or you can take me to it in the morning," I said. I leaned in and kissed him.

He grabbed the back of my head and pushed in for more kisses. The next thing I knew I was leaving the bar and I made sure Will saw me. I gave him a look of two can play that game. I blew a kiss to Will without Paul's knowledge and laughed. That was the last I remembered that night.

My eyes stung from the bright light shining on my face. I rolled over and realized I wasn't alone in my bed. As a matter of fact I wasn't even in my bed I was in Paul's bed. *Oh my god.* I shot upright and realized I was in my underwear. The pounding in my head told me I had way too much to drink. I pulled my legs into my chest. *Why with Paul? Of all people why him?* He rolled over and let out a big snore. I could not fathom what might have happened last night and ran towards the bathroom. My head throbbed with every foot I placed on the floor. I barely made it to the porcelain throne. My entire night of partying had come up and then some. I sat against the wall sweating and hating myself for doing this. *How could I have spent the night with Paul?*

Paul was the most arrogant man I have met. He is handsome but no Will. He was so incredibly rude and arrogant. This might be why he has been after me since I started working for Will. I had always been so careful not do irresponsible things like this. Paul waited for me to wear down. He saw me as his challenge. He hunted me like his prey until he found me in my bout of weakness and pounced on me literally.

The real problem is I am in love with Will and should have just been honest with him and I wouldn't be in this mess. I should have never taken the job either but I needed it. I would not be in Paul's bathroom puking and hating myself if I hadn't. I racked my brain trying to remember how I got here last night. The only thing I could think of was Will. I closed my eyes and rubbed my sore temples still in just my underwear. The cold floor sent shivers to my sick body. The urge to throw up shot my body back up hovering over the toilet. I flushed the toilet and turned the sink on cold water. I cupped my hands and splashed the water onto my face. I caught a glimpse of my reflection and started to cry. I thought my luck had changed and I would not be a victim to love anymore. I heard a noise outside the bathroom. *Paul.* He must have heard me in here vomiting. I dried my face off with a towel that was hanging by the door. I searched for toothpaste behind the mirror. I squeezed a bit onto my index finger for a make do tooth brush. A knock at the door startled me causing me to jump.

"Just a minute," I said.

"Hey, Gemma....I hope that you will not mention what happened last night. I am usually coherent," Paul said in a low voice. My shoulders relaxed after he said that.

I cracked the door and poked my head outside of it.

"Could you hand me my clothes please?" I asked. Just looking at him standing there rubbing his hands together in his boxers I knew he was ashamed of himself. That made two us.

He shook his head and picked up pieces of my clothes that were scattered around the room. He handed them through the door and looked at me in the eyes. "Gemma, this is not how I pictured us hooking up," Paul said with sadness in his eyes.

"Well, I thought we didn't hook up," I said. *God I hope we didn't do anything.*

Paul looked down at the floor and said, "We were getting really hot and heavy and then I blacked out."

"How did I get here?" I asked.

"All of us met up at Mackey's Pub. You were looking so good last night and you were all relaxed until Will showed up with some chick. You started pounding drinks and kissing on me," Paul said." I couldn't have been happier,"

I rolled my eyes, "I was kissing on you?"

"Ask anyone at the bar. One thing I should tell you though," he said rubbing the back of his neck.

"What?" I asked.

"When Will saw you leaving with me, he said something about you," he said.

My heart jumped into my throat. I remembered whom he was there with. It was Julie, my former roommate and a backstabbing slut. My face warmed and I grabbed my clothes from Paul and put them on. They smelled of cigarettes and booze, just another reminder of how much fun I was going to have or how much pain I was in.

"So, what did Will say to you then?" I said with the door still closed.

I heard Paul clear his throat; "He said to tell you not to bother to show up for work tomorrow."

I started laughing. Don't bother showing up for work. I planned on never going back. I started to remember little things of the night. I wanted to cry but not in front of Paul. I grabbed my purse and searched for my phone. I had several missed calls and text messages.

"Paul, Thank you for being honest with me. I have to go," I said heading towards the front door of his apartment.

He still stood in his boxers. He was very comfortable in his own skin even at his most vulnerable. I admired him for that. I was happy that we hadn't hooked up but I still had been here in my underwear close to it. I was a fool. The worst part is now I was starting to remember pieces of the night. I didn't say anything else to him and left.

I walked out of Paul's apartment building looking at my phone and threw it back in my purse. Tears rolled down my face. My body ached from the pain I felt from seeing Will with Julie. He fired me because I went home with Paul. He was so double standard. He made me feel more like his friend with benefits more than anything. The pain I felt in my chest was unbearable. I walked slowly; barely able to see where I was with the tears in my eyes. I wiped my tears on my arm and noticed I was downtown. Paul lived in a swanky part of town not far from Will. *What a joke this was.* I had made such a fool out of myself. I kept my head down as I walked to the bus station.

I stood in line waiting for a bus ticket thinking about those hurtful memories. *How could Will show up to Mackey's with Julie. I trusted him. I told him about how much she had done to me in just a few months of living with her.* Will looked good as he usually does but last night was different. I wanted him not Paul. I wanted him to be jealous and stop

Paul from hitting on me while I was drunk. The whole thing made my stomach churn. In a few hours, I will be out of here and in Richmond with my best friend Maxine to try to pick up the piece.

Chapter 18

Bus rides

"Next," a voice yelled, waking me out of my trance. The line for bus tickets had moved slowly but it was already my turn. "What can I do for you young lady?" said the bus ticket agent. She stood behind a wall with a computer and glass that separated us. She was older in her fifties. She probably had been doing this for some time now because the other agents would ask her for help. Her hair was sprinkled with grays and browns. Her eyes tightened with crow's feet when she talked.

"Can I get a one way ticket to Richmond Virginia?" I asked still staring at her features.

She typed in her computer to see the schedule. She looked up from her glasses and said, "The next bus to Richmond will not be for another two hours is that ok?" the lady said.

I shook my head and said yes.

"That will be forty five dollars ma'am," she said looking me over.

I handed her my check card not even thinking that anyone might trace me back to here. That is if they wanted to find me. Deep in my heart I wanted Will to find me and take me away from all this craziness. I signed the receipt and grabbed my tickets and looked for a seat. I found one looking out the tinted window. That was my temporary residence until they call for my bus. I was heading towards Richmond where I had visited my friend Maxine many times. I would visit her on breaks and she would visit me. She had been trying to convince me to move there after college. I decided this would be a better time more than ever to take her up on her offer. She was the kind of girl that didn't ask too many questions. She accepted me with my flaws even though she didn't always agree with me. I thought to call her that I was coming but I would once I got closer to her.

My head still throbbed from my drunken escapade last night. I desperately could not wait for a shower. I wanted to wash off Paul's scent and start fresh. It was making me ill. My eyes burned from the thought that I could have really messed up more than I did. I closed my eyes and rubbed my temples

A smile stretched on my face when my mind took me back to the first day working for Will.

A voice broke out over the intercom announcing the bus to Richmond was now boarding. I walked in a trance not really caring about that I had left my clothes, my car, and my life behind. I would only be three hours away. It was still close enough to my brother that if he needed me I could ride the bus back. I knew at this point he would be furious with me. I have relied on him like my dad since he left us. Nate went to school and got a fancy job and sent mom home money and extravagant gifts. He didn't pay for my college but insisted that I go to a good one so I could have a better future.

I handed the driver my ticket and found a seat in the middle of the bus. I only had my purse with me so no need to worry about cramping a suitcase under the bus. I skimmed the people to see who was boarding. The bus driver roared up the bus after about ten minutes. My phone vibrated in my purse.

I searched my purse for phone. Will's face and name flashed on the id. It was the only picture I got of him and used for my phone. I hit a button sending him to voice mail. I desperately wanted to hear his voice but it would just hurt too much. He should have never been with Julie last night. I gazed at my phone and his face disappeared. I leaned my head on the tinted bus window and closed my eyes. I felt safe enough knowing I was getting the hell out of here. The bus barely had twenty people on it. I drifted back into thoughts of Will.

The bus rolled over a bump causing me to almost fall onto the dirty floor. I knew I had not showered but I didn't want to tempt fate any further. An older couple sat a few seats in front of me. They argued over where he put his glasses and how she was stubborn, I couldn't help but to smile. I checked the time on my phone and saw numerous missed calls and texts. Most of them from my brother, some from Will, and now one from Paul. I checked the texts first since they were easier to attend to. Nate kept asking me where I was and to call him. Will told me to call him a.s.a.p. Paul also decided that I should I call him immediately.

A robot voice indicated that I had seven missed calls. The first call was Nate reminding me how stupid I was for last night and blowing my job. Then, he called back to say sorry and to call him when I get his call. The next few were from Will. His voice was irritated he told me that he was disappointed in my decision to go home with Paul. He said we could discuss work arrangements later. I rolled my eyes at the audacity of him. *Really? Why the hell would I want to work with that asshole anymore?* He never should have came into Mackey's with Julie. If he wanted to hurt me and get me to quit he got what he wanted then.

I erased messaged along the way. Will's voice came back onto my phone. He sounded much different than his first message. He said to please call him or

Nate so that he would know if I were okay and he said in a low voice that he still loved me. Tears enveloped in my eyes. I wasn't going to cry over him anymore. I was still hurt and I was mad and disgusted with myself. Last but not least was a message from Paul. He didn't sound all creepy like usual but more concerned. He said he didn't know what the hell I was doing but I should contact Nate or Will soon. They are freaking out.

My fingers hovered over the phone and I pressed them to the letters.

~I am safe.

I sent my message to Nate. There was too much to say to Will and I couldn't dare send it in a text. I wasn't ready to talk to him and I didn't know if I would ever be ready. He could be with any girl but, why with the girl who was out to destroy me? My phone buzzed and the caller id flashed my brother's stupid face. I hesitated and touched the button to receive the call and place the phone to my ear.

"Hello," I said keeping my eyes out the window and my finger over my other ear.

The voice wasn't Nate's it was Will. "Don't hang up. I need to know you are all right. Where are you Gemma?" he said. I could hear the pain in his voice.

"I….am okay. I quit," I said and hung up the phone.

I hit the phone into my head. This is all I could think of to say to Will. I really was the stupidest person in the world. We had only been on the road for any hour and I was getting sick from the previous events and the bus fumes. I was thankful that the bus driver took a break at a stop for buses. I tried to find food in the closest vending machine and a drink. I relieved the pressure off my bladder and boarded back in the bus. During my break I received another call from Will. I held the phone to my ear listened to his sweet voice.

"Why are you headed to Richmond? What is there for you?" he asked and he was gone.

How the hell did he know I was going to Richmond? Then it dawned on me I paid for my ticket with my debit card. That sneaky bastard was having me tracked. I knew he was good at his job but I didn't know how well.

I texted him and said,

~Where I go is no longer your concern. I am no longer your employee.

It felt good to finally stand up for myself. I cut my phone off. I didn't want to hear anymore from him or my brother Nate. In about an hour I would be starting new a life in Richmond. I couldn’t wait to have a shower and a hot cup of tea. My heavy eyes closed and I tried not to think of his voice but it was inescapable.

What's Next?

Book 2

Hope you enjoyed Gemma and Will's story. Find out what happens when she gets to Richmond, VA and things get way more complicated. Book 2 should be out around early 2015.

10837317R00139

Printed in Great Britain
by Amazon.co.uk, Ltd.,
Marston Gate.